Life As I Knew It

Life As I Knew It

RANDI HACKER

Randi Hacker (signature)

Simon Pulse
New York   London   Toronto   Sydney

SIMON PULSE

An imprint of Simon & Schuster Children's Publishing Division

1230 Avenue of the Americas, New York, NY 10020

Copyright © 2006 by Randi Hacker

All rights reserved, including the right of reproduction in whole or in part in any form.

SIMON PULSE and colophon are registered trademarks of Simon & Schuster, Inc.

Designed by Karin Paprocki

The text of this book was set in Bembo.

Manufactured in the United States of America

First Simon Pulse edition October 2006

2 4 6 8 10 9 7 5 3 1

Library of Congress Control Number 2005020961

ISBN-13: 978-1-4169-0995-8

ISBN-10: 1-4169-0995-8

For Grandmother

Breakfast

❧❦❧

My name is Angelina Rossini. I am sixteen years old. I live in Blodgett, Vermont, a small town that, nonetheless, has two post offices—one in Blodgett Center and one in Blodgett Village, a mere two and a quarter miles away. The postmistress despots of these post offices are engaged in a long-term feud, neither one willing to merge with the other, despite the fact that the sum total of the population of both areas is a whopping 854. It's quite Shakespearean, actually. I mean, listen to this: When the son of the postmistress from Blodgett Center married the daughter of the postmistress from Blodgett Village, it was like *Romeo and Juliet, Way Down North*. The postmistresses, despite being in-laws, still don't speak to each other. And, ohmigod! I can't wait to see what happens when the first grandchild is born. I am not alone in this.

Anyway.

In a town with this level of eccentricity, people like my parents do not stand out. Well, not that much.

My father's name was Andrea Rossini, and he came to the United States back in the sixties from a small town in Italy called Sforzato, which is very hard for Americans to say. He came as a salesman for a pretty big Italian import/export concern, then he worked his way up to CEO. He retired about five years ago. A very nice executive salary on top of a generous retirement, including shares in the company, along with some shrewd investments, made us if not independently wealthy, then at least independently self-sustaining. My father was sixty-nine when he died.

My mother's name is Nicola. She's British and has a very posh accent. This means that no matter what she says, whether it's a poem by Robert Browning or "Angelina, you look like a slob," you want her to say it again. She is fifty-eight.

Do the math and you'll see that my parents were quite old when they had me. In fact, my mother thought she couldn't have children at all. They'd tried and tried, and had concluded, after many years, that she was infertile. Barren. Nonfecund. I looked all these words up when I was thirteen after a particularly bad fight with my mother when I was actually wishing she had remained barren.

I suspect she was wishing that at the time too.

More about my parents:

My mother was thirty-six when she met my father, a divorcé. They entered into a torrid affair. Even though it is fairly icky to imagine that your parents were ever hot for each other, it isn't that hard to believe about my folks; they have always been totally into each other and formed something of a monolithic unit long before I ever came on the scene.

When my mother was forty-two, she and my father went to the state fair. They walked around the exhibits, ate corn dogs and pepper and sausage hoagies, maybe some fry bread or cotton candy, and, presumably, held hands in the moonlight on the midway. On a spur-of-the-moment decision they took a ride on the Centripede, one of those rides where the cars go totally around a loop and for one brief moment you are hanging upside down two hundred feet from the ground with nothing but a nylon webbing seat belt between you and death, asking yourself how you could have been so incredibly stupid to have gotten on this ride in the first place. Well—and this is a family legend, mind you—the ride malfunctioned while my father and mother were on it, and they ended up hanging upside down by their nylon webbing seat belts for a good half hour before they were rescued by emergency workers in a cherry picker. My father laughs when he tells this story. My mother still trembles and turns pale. Nevertheless, two months later she was pregnant. I like to think the Centripedal force and inversion shook that egg that was half me right out of its ovarian solitary confinement.

A little bit more about my dad:

In the way that Scarlett O'Hara was not really beautiful, my father was not really handsome, but no one noticed on account of all the charm he gave off. You would think that because he was so charming, he'd have been really popular. He wasn't. When it came to my father, people either loved him or hated him—sometimes both in the same day.

But no one, absolutely no one, in Blodgett *didn't* know who he was.

He was quite a large presence here in our small town. He was the only Italian national, for starters, and every fall, on Town Market Day, he would go all Sicilian and sing arias and fling pizza dough around like a commercial for Andrea's Authentic Old Italian Pizza or something. One of the greatest photos I have is of him in his gondolier's hat, a red bandanna tied around his neck, brandishing a pizza slicer, a wicked grin on his face.

About Town Market Day:

This is the day in the fall when Blodgett reinvents itself as Vermontworld. Every small and not-so-small Vermont town has a similar day: Old Home Day, Old Settlers' Day, Down Home Day, Hometown Day, etc. Basically it's Vermonters selling Vermont to non-Vermonters. Kinda hokey, I know, but it pulls the town together in a very seventies way, which is not surprising, since a lot of Blodgett's population is made up of graying hippies who went ex-urban back then.

On Town Market Day in Blodgett, Vermont, there are sidewalk sales, a fire department chicken barbecue, a band, games for kids at the rec center, and a horse parade voted best in the state by either *Vermont* or *Vermont Life* magazine; I always get them confused.

My father secretly called ours Town Marketing Day, and though he liked to make fun of it, he had fun at it too. I think it appealed to his inner salesman.

It *can* be fun.

Anyway.

I never learned Italian. My mother doesn't speak it, and so the two of them decided, long before I had any lips, that English would be spoken here. Very British, very much the Empire at Work. I think my mother did not want to be left out of any interaction my father had with me.

I think he always thought he'd teach me at a later date.

My father loved to talk and readily gave his opinion whether it was asked for or not. More often than not his opinions were insightful and sardonic. Sometimes they were stupid. But they were always forcefully presented.

But I'm getting ahead of myself, and I really want to tell this story in order.

So.

It was morning. Our house was in its usual morning mode. I was dawdling in my closet. What to wear? Something "presentable" . . . or something that would bug my mother? Always a tough fashion decision. I could hear her downstairs in the kitchen and smell the coffee she was brewing. She makes a great cup of coffee, I'll give her that.

"Angelina!" she called. "Come on!"

I slipped into a pair of jeans with a big hole in the

knee, and a pretty tight black ribbed wifebeater with 安, a Chinese character for peace, on it. I really wanted to have this tattooed on my right shoulder blade, but the folks were dead set against it, and I still haven't had the nerve to have it done on the sly. Yet.

I pulled on a baggy, shapeless, formerly blue sweater that I don't even really remember buying, slipped my feet into a pair of pink plastic flip-flops, and looked in the mirror.

I looked okay.

I heard frantic barking outside, so I looked out my window. Down below on the patio, Mokey, our little terrier, was terrorizing a squirrel in a tree.

I opened the window a crack and called out, "Get 'im, Mokey!"

Mokey is not the brightest bulb in the chandelier, as evidenced by the fact that he runs right in front of any car that comes down our driveway. But he is cute. And he and my mother have one of those supernatural dog/ human connection things going on. I mean, he likes me, but basically he's her love slave.

When he heard my voice, he looked up at me, then disappeared under the overhang. I heard him scrabble at the French doors, heard the doors open, and then heard his toenails skittering on the polished wood of the stairs. Shortly afterward he burst into my room, where he executed the full body wag of total love, then peed on the floor.

Eeeuw.

Suddenly I heard a roar from below. I scooped Mokey up and ran downstairs. The sight that greeted me was straight out of one of those black-and-white screwball comedies me and my mom always watched together when I was younger and my dad was gone on business all week.

My father was standing in front of the French doors; little drops slipped through the spaces between the planks of the ceiling and dripped onto his head. I should probably mention here that my room is directly above the dining room and we live in an old farmhouse. Spaces between the wide-plank floorboards are considered to have rustic charm. And they do. But the laws of physics prevail even in the presence of high levels of rustic charm.

So, in accordance with the laws of physics, the pee had dripped down from my room onto my father's head as he stood in his morning attire—old flannel nightshirt, bare feet, yellowish white bedhead hair—in the dining room.

True story.

So.

Anyway.

I bit my lips to keep from laughing and looked at my mother. She looked as if she was fighting laughter too. She took Mokey from me, and even though it was a little "closing the barn door after the horse has escaped"-ish, she opened the doors and put him out.

My father's face was red, red, red. My mother and I glanced at each other. We both braced ourselves for a possible explosion: Metaphorically speaking, we put our fingers in our ears, gritted our teeth, and squinched our eyes shut.

But instead of blowing up, my father laughed.

He laughed.

My mother and I looked at each other, and then we laughed too.

I remember this moment. It shines in my memory like a scene from *My Life: The Movie*. The all-star, all-time cast would be Sean Connery as my father, Lynn Redgrave as my mother, and Christina Ricci as me.

"Good morning, *cara mia*!" said my father, wiping his face with a paper towel that my mother had handed him.

"I will not kiss you until I have washed the pee out of my hair and beard."

As far as I was concerned, he could wash his beard all he wanted, but it would be a long time before I could kiss him again without shuddering!

"And this will be a good lesson for you in the ways of love," he said as he passed me. "Always . . . no, *never* kiss a man until he has washed the pee out of his hair and beard. And never kiss a man who pees in his own hair, even if he has washed it out!"

"Yuck. As if!" I said.

My father winked at me, said, "*Ti voglio bene*," threw a kiss to my mother, said, "*Ti amo*," and walked off toward the bathroom, singing at the top of his lungs, "Don't cry for me, Angelina. . . ."

Confession: You should know right now that my father and I are rabid Andrew Lloyd Webber fans. *Evita* is our favorite show of all. It's kind of a private joke between us that my name fits so perfectly into that song.

My mother gazed off after my father with an expression that showed that even after all these years—even with pee in his hair—she was still totally in love with him.

How embarrassing is that?

I have often wondered just what attracted my father to my mother. Her parts are not all that exceptional. Taken individually, her features are okay, but somehow, put all together, they don't quite add up to beauty. Her body's not bad. She's like a tiny Amazon: broad-shouldered, tapered waist and hips, long neck. Her legs are surprisingly shapely, and her feet are way tiny; I think she actually wears a 4½ and feels comfortable in them. I have very large feet. I didn't get them from her. I didn't get my thin, mousy brown hair from her either. Her hair is kind of fabulous—dark and thick and shiny, and she wears it chin length in a blunt cut. She colors it, but it's not one of those colors that you don't find on Earth. It's totally convincing.

Right—so all that about my mother's unconventional beauty said, every once in a while I *can* see just how totally attractive she can look. And it's not usually when she's all dolled up, either; sometimes when she comes in after raking or gardening, in old dirty clothes, her hair tied up in a bandanna, with a smudge of dirt on her face and a spot behind her ear bleeding from a black-fly bite, she looks so . . . I don't know, attractive. Sexy, even. *Then* I can see what might be there between them, which can be pretty icky, as I've said, but also kind of hopeful. I mean, I guess I've got good reason to believe that true love really exists. Certainly when I see her face all glowing like that, I almost know. She's almost pretty then, and there's a softness about her that isn't usually there—at least not when she's dealing with me these days.

Now that my father was out of the room, my mother turned her attention to me. She gave me the once-over.

"Why do you insist on wearing such shapeless clothes, Angelina?" she said. "And it's too cold for flip-flops."

"I'm not cold," I said—though, in truth, my toes *were* a little chilly.

"When are you going to learn how to . . . ," began my mother.

It was lecture number bazillion in a never-ending series.

But this time she never finished, because at that moment there was a crash in the bathroom, followed by a long, low inhuman sound.

A Vision of Heaven

M y mother sprinted for the bathroom.
"Andrea? Andrea!"

I just froze. I mean, I just stood there until the sound of Mokey's barking and scratching at the glass got a little too frantic. I let him in and he made a beeline for the bathroom, skittering on the wood as he took the hardwood corner on two paws.

I closed the patio doors extra quietly. . . .

"Angelina! Call 911!" my mother shouted.

And that sort of snapped me out of it. I picked up the wall phone, punched in the three numbers, then stretched the cord to the max and looked into the bathroom too.

I'll never forget what I saw.

Never.

My father lay on the floor, still.

Seeing him so still was more than scary: It was just wrong.

Even wronger was his face. It was blank; his cheeks were lax; his mouth was slack. It was as if he had gone somewhere and left his head behind.

Except for his eyes. His eyes were pinpoints of panic. Pure panic.

My mother was curiously calm. She washed his face with a washcloth, held his hand, stroked his hair, and whispered to him.

The 911 voice answered and drew my attention away from the scene. Giving the woman our address felt weird. It was like I was totally outside my registration lines—like Sylvester the cat after he's been hit in the face with a frying pan. *Boioioinnnnng!*

"It's my father," I said, working the words through my lips.

She took my address and said, "We're on our way."

"I'm scared," I said.

But she had already hung up.

A note about small-town life in the twenty-first century: Not long ago when there was an emergency in Blodgett, you direct-dialed Billy Thibeault, EMT and school custodian, and he came with the old ambulance, which was parked in his driveway. Now we have a new ambulance parked in the new emergency building, where the old school used to be, and you have to call 911 central, who then calls Billy T., who drives from his house to the new emergency building, then drives the new ambulance to your house. In actuality it doesn't take that much longer, but it seems much stupider. Doesn't it?

"Fetch a blanket from the living room," my mother ordered in a soft but authoritative voice. She did not look at me. She continued to look at my father. I did as she asked, and helped her tuck the blanket around my father.

Drool leaked out of the corner of my father's mouth and ran down his cheek. My mother wiped it away gently with the hem of her nightgown, but not before Mokey licked some of it. At the touch of Mokey's tongue I thought I saw a flicker of something in my father's eyes— amusement? Bemusement? I don't know, but when I looked again, it was gone. Replaced by the panic I'd seen earlier.

"Stay beside him," said my mother. "I must dress." And so saying, she stood and left the bathroom, Mokey trotting behind her. Despite her wet hem and bare feet, she broadcast dignity and self-control. I loved and admired her then. I was feeling anything but dignified and self-controlled.

I sat down on the tiles next to my father. Spittle was leaking out of his mouth again, but try as I might, I could not bring myself to use my own clothing to wipe it away. What would it take for me to use an article of my own clothing—the clothing I was wearing—as a cleanup cloth? I wondered. I got a tissue and used that. Then, holding it gingerly between thumb and forefinger, I tossed it toward the trash can and missed.

I didn't pick it up.

His eyes were closed. I took his hand. It was limp, and his fingers did not squeeze back when I squeezed them, but he opened his eyes. I leaned close and placed my cheek against the stubble on his. He still smelled of the soap that my mother had used to wash his face.

"Don't die, Daddy," I whispered into his ear. "Please don't die." I felt tears slide down my cheeks and onto my father's face.

There was a knock at the door. Billy was here. I wiped my tears with the heel of my hand and stood up.

"I'll be right back, Daddy," I said, heading for the door. "Don't go away!"

Black humor. Sometimes it works. Sometimes it doesn't.

I looked out the window and saw Billy Thibeault, EMT and school custodian, standing on our front porch with his wife, Dorcas, ambulance driver and waitress (breakfast shift) at Sugar's, the local diner. Between them was the trolley stretcher. I opened the door and they rolled it in.

"He's in the bathroom," my mother said. She was descending the stairs, dressed neatly in a pair of tailored slacks, a blouse, and a cardigan. She had a pair of Italian loafers on her tiny feet. Her hair was combed, and she had her purse over her shoulder. All business.

We followed Team Thibeault into the bathroom and watched as they skillfully transferred my father from the tile floor to the trolley and secured him. Then we followed again as they rolled him back to the ambulance and loaded him in.

Before they shut the doors, I caught a glimpse of what was going on inside. My father blinked once at his surroundings, then shut his eyes. I wanted to say something— good-bye? No. See ya later? No. But before I could decide on what might be appropriate, the school bus pulled up.

My mother saw it, and it was as if she was suddenly reminded of me. She blinked and looked around, one foot in the ambulance and one foot on the gravel of the driveway. It took her a moment to locate me. Weird thing was, I was standing right there. Just off to the side. "Go to school," my mother said.

School? Was it a school day?

"You've got to be kidding!" I said.

"Go to school," she said firmly. She pulled her other leg into the ambulance. Dorcas shut the doors and climbed up behind the wheel. Billy rode shotgun. The ambulance turned around, pulled out of the driveway, and sped away down the hill in a cloud of dust.

We needed rain.

Numbly I turned and walked toward the bus.

Laila, the bus driver, opened the doors and waited patiently for me to put Mokey in his crate, retrieve my backpack, grab a cold Pop-Tart, and climb the embankment to the road. This is one of the advantages of living in a small town; the bus driver waits.

When I climbed aboard the bus, Laila patted my hand but didn't say anything. Since I am the first person to be picked up in the morning, I didn't have to deal with anyone else's reaction to the ambulance in my driveway. I was grateful for that, and I sank into a seat and closed my eyes. The bus lurched off.

I felt like I needed to do something, think something good for my father. Was a prayer in order? Try as I might, I couldn't think of what to pray for, so I settled for a succinct and understated "Help. Please." Then I leaned my forehead against the window and watched the fields and houses slip past.

Northern Vermont is mostly beautiful. Today the mountains were flecked with reds, and the sky was that autumn blue that looks colder than it is. Horses could still find green grass to eat, and you could still take your jacket off in the afternoon.

"I believe I speak for Vermont school bus drivers everywhere when I say that fall is like heaven for us," said Laila, putting the bus in gear and heading toward the Addamses' farm to pick up Kayla. "No ice. No mud. Just color and roads that could use a little grading. Heaven."

She looked at me in the rearview mirror and smiled a small smile.

If there is a heaven, I thought at the time, it must be totally different for everyone, only the thing that makes it heaven is that the realities never clash: I mean, everyone there experiences heaven in their own way, and yet they coexist happily because the differences don't matter because it's, well—it's heaven.

I hadn't thought about what my heaven might look like, but I knew one thing: It wouldn't have the memory of today in it.

That made me wonder what kind of heaven my father might envision, and I realized I had no idea. I pressed my forehead against the window and let it bang, bang, bang against the glass as the bus rolled down a road that could use a little grading here in Laila's heaven.

All Families Are Different

T*he first person I saw* in school was Jax Tatro. He was waiting for me at my locker. No big deal. Jax waits for me every morning. He's my best friend. We've been best friends since kindergarten when we sneaked under the table and cut each other's hair with the safety scissors.

"Sorry to hear about your dad," he whispered, throwing an arm over my shoulder.

I hugged him. He always smelled so good—turpentiny and like fresh air and wool. I didn't have to ask him how he knew already: Billy Thibeault is his mother's brother.

I nodded.

"My mother said to tell you you're welcome at our place after school," he said.

I nodded again. "Thanks, Jax." I threw my arm around his waist, and we walked to our first class. Since it was math, and since I had a lot on my mind, we walked extra slow.

My heaven would definitely include Jax's house—and everyone in it. He has to have one of the world's largest extended families. He's pretty much related to everyone in Blodgett Center somehow. He lives with his parents in a run-down old farmhouse on the main road between Blodgett Center and West Blodgett. His Granny Nancy and his great-grandmother, whom Jax just calls Great, live in a duplex apartment over the local video store. Great's seventy-eight—only nine years older than my father.

As I said, Jax's mother is Billy's sister. The bus driver is Jax's aunt by marriage, and at least two teachers in our school are cousins of his. And Jax had a couple of nieces in the lower grades too, until his brother Sean's wife left town with the kids.

Anyway.

Unlike Jax, I have no extended family really. My parents are so old their parents died before I was born. The generational matrix is still pretty dense, though: My half sister, Francesca, who is forty-two, lives in New Mexico with her son, Anthony, who is only six months younger than I am. Her husband is a day trader. I don't see them very often. And there is no love lost between Francesca and my mother for two reasons that I can think of:

1. My mom married her father.
2. My mom is only sixteen years older than she is.

Getting back to Jax, he and I have another thing in common. We both like boys. Jax hasn't come right out and told his folks about this yet; his father and 66 percent of his brothers are big-time loggers and lumbermen; they spit and smoke and drink and blow their noses without the benefit of a handkerchief or tissue. Jax doesn't think that they would fully grasp the whole "I'm here, I'm queer, get used to it" concept, and I tend to agree with him. I think his mother might suspect; she's very intuitive. But the only one who knows for sure—the only one he's actually told besides me, that is—is Granny Nancy, in whose eyes Jax can do no wrong. It's one of those Hollywood intergenerational bond things that you think happens only in movies. She's pretty cool. Just before she graduated high school, she met a draft-dodger from the U.S. and they ran off to live in a commune in Manitoba where she smoked a lot of dope, learned *batiking*, and picked up some hippie speak that she gave her own unique twist to—you haven't heard anything until you've heard her say "*Quel* bummer"; it comes out like "bow mare," which sounds a lot less negative, if you ask me. Eventually, she went back to Quebec, married her high school sweetheart, and raised a family. She ended up in Blodgett when her daughter, that's Jax's mother, immigrated here.

Anyway, Jax's dream is to blow this burb as soon as he graduates high school and move to L.A.—or more accurately, Hollywood—and make movies. To make money now he works weekends and summers for his family's logging and lumber operation driving skidders and forklifts and front loaders and big trucks. "Just because you're a fairy," Jax told me once, "doesn't mean you can't drive a big rig!"

Damn straight.

Here's something you should know right now: I love Jax. I mean, really. And he knows it. It's always been cool between us because we have had years to work it out and we respect each other's boundaries and blah, blah, blah. But every once in a while I still get the hots for him in a major way. Can't help it. His work makes him hard as steel. His muscles are a thing of beauty, and with his Abenaki ancestry showing in his bone structure and his deep-set dark eyes, he is heartbreakingly handsome. Seriously. I just know when he hits Melrose, he is going to be fighting the boys off with a stick. I already know what my going-away gift to him is going to be: a bucket of condoms.

So, right. He's my boy friend. But not my boyfriend. If you know what I mean.

I haven't ever had a real boyfriend—you know, one who reciprocates my desire to tear his clothes off—unless you count Jason Andrews, whose mother found us touching each other "down there" when we were three. And the chances of my having one anytime soon are slim to none: There are twenty-four kids in my class, and eighteen of them are girls.

I'm setting my sights on college.

Anyway.

When we got to the classroom, we found the doorway blocked by Celeste Larivee. Perhaps it was wishful thinking on her mother's part, but Celeste is about the least fitting name you could ever give to this girl. To me the name Celeste conjures up something light and airy, something celestial, like an angel. *This* Celeste is more heavy and gravity dependent. She's hefty, too, built like a linebacker, and pretty nasty. We used to be friends in elementary school, but we're not anymore. She's always had an attitude, but lately it's like it's on steroids. Don't know what's up with that.

"You're late, faggot!" said Celeste to Jax. She likes to

use names like this for Jax, even though she's just guessing.

"Let us in, Celeste," I said.

"Look who's here too," she sneered. "The girl with grandparents for parents. How are your senior citizens this morning? Did you adjust their hearing aids for them? Make sure their walkers are close at hand in case they need to shuffle to the bathroom to fix their dentures while you're in math?"

Whoa.

"Just because your mother still uses Clearasil," I said, "is no reason to be proud."

Celeste's mother is thirty-three, her grandmother is forty-nine, and her great-grandmother is sixty-six. Her great-great-grandmother would be pushing eighty-four if she hadn't bit the big one last year in a freak accident involving a snowmobile and a six-pack.

"Oh yeah?" said Celeste. "Well, at least I don't have to change her Depends!"

Now, on a normal morning I might have shaken all of this off. On a normal morning I might have sighed with resignation, shaken my head with pity, and pushed past her into the classroom. On a normal morning I might have rolled my eyes at Jax and maybe even laughed in a superior fashion. "Ha, ha, ha!"

But this was *not* a normal morning.

So I jumped her.

Celeste outweighs me by at least twenty pounds, but the attack was so unexpected that I caught her off balance and she came down like a felled tree. Pretty soon we were rolling around on the indoor-outdoor carpeting in the math classroom, tearing at each other's hair and grunting. Jax kept trying to pull me off her. Everyone else just egged us on.

"Fight! Fight! Fight! Fight! Fight!" they chanted.

Celeste scraped her filthy fingernails across my cheek and I managed to land one or two good punches to her meaty stomach before Mr. Crispi pulled us apart. Celeste's nose, I was gratified to see, was bleeding. My own face felt hot and raw. I put my hand up to my cheek and winced. There was blood on my fingertips. I ran my tongue over my teeth—nothing broken, thank God. Three thousand dollars' worth of orthodontic work would be an awfully high price to pay for a fight with such a loser.

"To the principal's office, both of you," said Mr. Crispi. "And the rest of you, to your seats."

"What's the magic word, Mr. C.?" asked Jason.

"Now!" said Mr. C.

Everyone laughed and found their seats. Celeste and I moved stealthily toward our seats too, but . . .

"Ms. Larivee and Ms. Rossini," said Mr. C., "perhaps you two did not hear me. You two are to go to the principal's office."

"I didn't do any—," Celeste started to say, but even she wasn't stupid enough to think this would work with the gashes on my cheeks bleeding freely. I saw Celeste's big, slow brain shift gears—I almost heard the machinery grind to a halt, then start up sluggishly again.

"She started it!" said Celeste triumphantly.

"To the office!" said Mr. Crispi, pulling at the knot in his SpongeBob SquareTie.

I glanced at Jax, who grimaced at me. He mouthed, "Later," and I nodded.

I looked at my watch; 8:36 a.m. Barely an hour had passed since my father collapsed.

And now I was on my way to the principal's office.

If the morning was any indication of how the rest of the day was going to shape up, I just hoped I could survive until lunch.

Sighing, I hefted my pack and followed my nemesis out the door.

The Fine Line Between Embarrassing and Cool

❧❦❧

"H ave a seat, girls," said Mrs. Percy as Celeste and I slouched into the office a few minutes later. She indicated the wooden chairs on either side of the mail-boxes, then went back to her typing. Celeste and I sat down and waited. The way the chairs were set up, we couldn't even see each other when we leaned back—and that was just fine with me. I put my pack between my ankles and closed my eyes. The first thing I saw with my eyes closed was my father lying helpless on the bathroom floor, though, so I immediately snapped them open again and looked at Mrs. Percy instead.

Mrs. Percy is the school secretary, and she's either totally embarrassing or she's totally cool. Or maybe she's both. It's hard to tell. She's a skinny marink with a totally retro look. Her hair is always up in a beehive, and it's a color not naturally occurring on this planet. I always worry about the aquifer when I notice she's touched up her roots again. She wears vintage cat-eye glasses—leopard-print frames on a pearl chain. In summer capri pants are her uniform. In the winter she's got a fake-fur jacket—also leopard print—and a collection of shirtwaists in pastel colors. To complete her look, she has a leopard-print steering wheel cover and a pair of foam rubber dice hanging from the rearview mirror of her classic Ford Mustang. Given all this, her footgear is something of a surprise: Mrs. Percy wears hiking boots. With everything—and I mean everything. For example, at Adam Levy's bar mitzvah she showed up in a green cocktail dress and hiking boots.

"If your feet aren't comfortable, *you* aren't comfortable," she says.

It didn't look that bad, actually. She has a way of making unexpected fashion combos work.

Mrs. Percy is also something of a local celebrity as her alter ego, Sugar the career waitress. She's the image and inspiration behind Sugar's, the local diner. In fact, she used to own it but sold out at what she likes to refer to as a "tidy little profit," and now she makes only a weekly

Sunday appearance there as part of a town fund-raiser.

Sugar's is a retro diner. The fittings are totally authentic twentieth-century golden age of diners stuff: Formica tabletops with matching vinyl booth upholstery, individual jukeboxes at every booth, a chrome-railed counter with three stools, and a big analog clock ringed in pink and blue neon over the doorway to the kitchen. Even the muffin display case dates back to 1954.

Sugar's has been featured in *Banquette* and *Over Easy*, the two top trade magazines in dinerdom. Three times. With pics.

No one in Blodgett is surprised. No matter what objections the townspeople may have to her personality quirks, it is universally agreed that her taste is fab.

As I said, Sugar shows up at Sugar's every Sunday morning—sort of like a performance art piece with a weekly time slot. The thing is, no one knows what time she'll show up. That's the game. People go to Sugar's and predict what time she'll show up. Whoever comes closest gets their breakfast free. Catch Sugar, it's called. It's a dollar a guess, and the proceeds go to support town enterprises like the work of the rec department or the town library.

My father loved playing Catch Sugar when guests came from out of town. Going to Sugar's and playing this game gave my father the opportunity to show off the town's character and his own character in one fell swoop.

When his older brother, my uncle Giancarlo, came from Italy, we did the Sugar thing—Andrea style. That meant maintaining two things: (1) low anxiety and (2) a leisurely pace. I was about eleven back then, though, and the concept of a leisurely pace had no place in my life.

"But Daddy!" I cried. "She could show up anytime from six a.m. to noon. If we don't get there till nine, we'll miss three hours of possible entry times!"

"*Calmex, cara mia,*" said my father, using an expression he'd invented to say to me when I got hopped up. "As my father used to say, *que sera, sera:* 'If it's meant to be, it will be.'"

"Our father never said that," Uncle Giancarlo told my father.

"No?" my father answered. He turned to my mother. "Did your father say that, then?" he asked her.

"Not once that I can recall," said my mother, smiling. "Of course, I'm pretty old now and can't always remember childhood with the clarity I once did."

My father put his arm around my mother and pulled her to him.

"You, old? Never, *cara mia*," he said, and kissed her cheek. "You are my young wife, my Nicola."

I shook my eleven-year-old head and rolled my eleven-year-old eyes.

"Get a room!" I said.

I remember we all laughed.

We finally got to Sugar's at 9:00 a.m. It was crowded, but when you live in northern Vermont, the word "crowded" takes on an entirely different meaning: six of the nine booths were taken, as were two of the three stools.

Dorcas came out of the kitchen balancing breakfasts on both arms. She saw us, smiled, and indicated a booth in the corner with her chin. Lesley Gore was on the jukebox. The smell of bacon was in the air. I breathed deeply, then went to check out the Catch Sugar board.

I saw that Kevin Murphy, master plumber and adjunct professor of political science at Green Mountain Community College, had taken 9:34. I looked around and spotted him seated at the counter reading the paper. *Sucker!* I thought. Way too early.

Another family came in and stood behind me. I

glanced at them: strangers. I let them go first. They chose 9:47. A good time, but not a *great* time; my gut told me to choose a time closer to 10:00. They moved on. I looked back at the chart.

So, 9:56 or 9:58. Which one? I closed my eyes to see if either one of them appeared in my brain in numbers of fire. Nope. I opened my eyes and chose 9:58.

I wrote our name, Rossini, on the line next to that time, then wrote the time on a little red ticket and put our dollar in the kitty. I joined my party at our booth.

Dorcas sped by and dropped menus on the table. I didn't need a menu. I had what I always had: feta and broccoli omelet, homemade toast, and home fries. My father had what he always had: eggs over easy with sausage. My mom ordered eggs Benedict, and my uncle tried the Texas omelet. The adults ordered coffee, and I got hot chocolate.

I don't know what the adults talked about. I watched the clock and the door.

At 9:23 the party at the table across from us ripped up their red ticket, paid for their breakfast, and left.

At 9:29 our food came.

At 9:34 Kevin ripped up his ticket, dropped it in his

empty coffee mug, folded the paper, nodded to us, and walked out.

At 9:47 the family that had come in after me ceremonially drowned their ticket in leftover maple syrup.

At 9:52 I put down my fork and knife. Who could eat with all the suspense?

The seconds ticked by on the big clock over the kitchen doorway.

I began chewing on my nails.

"*Calmex*, my little Angelina," said my father. "*Que sera, sera*: 'If it is meant to be, it will be.' Say, did we ever determine whose father it was that said this?"

"You say it, Daddy," I said, never taking my eyes from the door.

"I knew it was someone's father," said my father. He laughed. I didn't. I just continued to stare at the door.

At 9:58 Sugar walked in. She was dressed in a lime green waitress's shirtwaist with apron, hiking boots, support hose, much costume jewelry, and her cat-eye glasses. Her beehive was hidden underneath a leopard-print kerchief. She checked the board, turned and looked for us, and smiled. She took her kerchief off, stowed her purse beneath the cash register, grabbed a coffeepot, and headed our way.

"Refills, anyone?" she asked.

Dorcas took a Polaroid of us, and three minutes later our picture joined all the other winners' and celebs' on the Sugar Wall. She tacked ours up between the photo of Sugar with Lauren Hutton and the photo of Sugar with Dr. Dean.

Plus we got our breakfast for free.

That was a good morning. Definitely heaven material.

Today Mrs. Percy was wearing a pink poodle skirt and a short-sleeved white blouse, and had a powder pink cashmere cardigan draped over her shoulders and fastened at the collar with one of those pearly clip things so popular in the days of June Cleaver. And of course she had on her hiking boots. With white bobby socks.

I leaned forward and looked at Celeste. I thought maybe the two of us could exchange a little smile about Mrs. Percy's style, but she just glared at me.

"What are you lookin' at, fag hag?" she hissed.

"Now, girls," said Mrs. Percy, looking up from her computer screen, "I don't like to see this kind of conflict between two members of the same community. With all the unrest in the world today, don't you think a little peace is in order?"

She rummaged through her handbag—a see-through plastic number with a pink flamingo, a palm tree, and the words *Florida: The Sunshine State* written in script on it—and pulled out two coupons for a free coffee and doughnut combo at Sugar's.

"Now, you girls go down to the diner—Sugar's is a designated DMZ, you know. Sit in a booth, put on a song by Aretha, drink some coffee, eat a doughnut, and make peace. If everybody who had a conflict just sat across from one another in a booth in a diner and talked it out over coffee and homemade doughnuts, the world would be a better place, don't you agree?"

We took our coupons, and when Mrs. Percy turned back to her work, me and Celeste looked at each other, raised our eyebrows, and smiled in the shared feeling that Mrs. Percy was a loon. A lovable loon, but a loon nonetheless.

My judgment must've been compromised by the morning's extreme emotions, because I almost asked Celeste right then and there if we could just forget it all and make up. But Celeste recovered from our simpatico/compatico moment sooner than I did and gave me the finger. The door to the principal's office opened just in time for Mrs. Principal to catch her at it. Celeste looked at the floor.

Mrs. Principal is our principal.

Her real name is Mrs. Silverman, but back when I was in first grade, one of my troublemaking classmates (not Celeste) slipped up and called her Mrs. Principal one day, and it just stuck. Everyone's called her that ever since. Some classes leave their alma mater a stone bench with something like CLASS OF '02 sandblasted on the backrest; our class left this nickname. It's our legacy to future BHS alums.

Anyway.

This being morning, I was surprised to see Mrs. Principal in her office. In the grand tradition of small towns, people generally tend to double up on jobs. For example, there's Billy T. and Sugar, whom you already know about; Ed Gantry, sheriff and electrician; and Gwen Paronto, video store owner and town dog warden. Our principal is also the first-grade teacher. She splits the jobs half and half. In the morning, she "principals," and her class is taught by her team teacher. In the afternoon, she teaches. It was clear from both her presence and her face that the gravity of the situation was such that she had been called to her principal's duties early.

I watched to see how Mrs. Principal would react to Celeste's gesture.

She looked at Celeste. She looked at me. She sighed, then she said, "Let's talk, girls," and we followed her into the inner sanctum.

Body is My Second Language

❧⟨❀⟩☙

Mrs. *Principal's office is very quiet.* Maybe it's the carpeting or the tasteful prints hanging on her walls. Or maybe it's just Mrs. Principal herself. She emits quiet vibes. She's calm and tall and somewhat unapproachable, though not unkind, if you know what I mean. You've got to respect Mrs. Principal, but you don't have to be afraid of her. At least not always.

If you've really stepped out of line, Mrs. Principal is a force to be reckoned with. I remember in eighth grade when Marcel Robidoux came to school drunk out of his mind. Mrs. Principal's wrath was silent but so powerful that Marcel seemed to shrink about six inches when she confronted him in the hallway, then suspended him for a week. But if you're just, like, a normal, good person, Mrs. Principal exudes a pleasant air of bemused tolerance.

Maybe it's an age thing.

Anyway, Mrs. Principal invited us to sit down at her round table. She's totally egalitarian. I remember having lunch at this table back in elementary school. She makes a point of inviting kids to eat with her through the years. Mrs. P. is one of those principals who gets involved.

Celeste dropped into her seat with an audible thud and crossed her arms over her chest.

Body language alert! *Whoop! Whoop! Whoop!*

I deliberately sat down more demurely. My mother would have been proud of the way I crossed my legs at the ankles, folded my hands in my lap, and maintained a non-threatening expression on my face.

"Okay, girls, let's have it," said Mrs. P., sitting down, putting her elbows on the table, and lacing her fingers together in front of her face. I noticed she had a French manicure. Unchipped. Pretty amazing for a woman who lives on a dairy farm. She fixed us with the famous Silverman Stare of Truth over the top of her reading glasses. No one could lie when bathed in the rays of the Silverman Stare of Truth. . . .

"I didn't do anything," sniveled Celeste.

Except Celeste.

I concentrated on breathing. In and out.

Mrs. P. said nothing. She ramped it up a notch, adding the Power of the Silent Void to the Stare of Truth. After fifteen years as the principal of a K–12 school she had this maneuver down to a science.

Pretty soon Celeste cracked.

"She jumped me!" said Celeste.

Mrs. P. nodded.

"She punched me in the nose," Celeste continued.

Mrs. P. looked at me. She took in the wounds on my cheek, no longer bleeding but still pretty raw.

"She's always making cracks about my parents' age," I said, a little whinier than I had actually planned. "And this morning I snapped."

Mrs. P. nodded.

"And then she made a crack about *my* family!" said Celeste.

"Served you right!" I shouted. "You impugned the ability of my parents to take care of their own bodily functions!" I wasn't sure if Celeste knew what "impugned" meant (I wasn't sure *I* knew, but it sounded good).

Mrs. P. stood up.

"Girls, there are all kinds of families in this world," she

said. "We do not choose our families; we just make the best of them. This is a universal truth among humans and probably has been for roughly thirty-five thousand years."

Whoa. Mrs. P. must have read *The Clan of the Cave Bear* once too often.

"We must not judge others for doing what we all do; and that is simply trying to live with one another," she continued. "Now, I want you to apologize to each other, then wash your faces and return to class, and I don't want to hear about this kind of behavior again, do you understand?"

Silence.

"Well?" said Mrs. P.

"Sorry I jumped you," I mumbled.

"Sorry . . . ," said Celeste, standing up. As she walked by me, she added under her breath, ". . . your folks are such geezers!" then she practically ran out of the room. I launched myself from the chair and was halfway to the door when I heard Mrs. P. say:

"Sit."

So I sat.

"I had a call from your mother," said Mrs. P. "From the hospital. The news is not good." She studied me over the top of her specs. It was a look that successfully mixed appraisal, sympathy, patience, wisdom, and quiet competence without being invasive. It must have taken her years to perfect. The half-glasses really helped lend it authority and dignity. If there were a reality show about principals, Mrs. Principal would not be voted off the island.

Okay, I'm rambling. Truth is, her words hit me hard, and I was rapidly approaching panic mode.

She pushed the phone across her desk.

"Would you like to call your mother?" she asked. "I've got the number right here." She handed me a small piece of paper with a phone number written on it.

Now, you'd think I'd jump at the chance—but instead I wondered, *Would I?* I kind of liked my own private reality—you know, the one in which I didn't think about Dad.

"I don't know. I mean, no. I mean, not now," I said.

Mrs. P. pulled the phone back toward her and said, "You can call her later if you like. Feel free to use my phone."

I nodded and stood, and then Mrs. Principal did something she hadn't done since I was in first grade and won the Dependability Award: She hugged me.

And I did something I hadn't done since first grade either: I hugged her back.

Lunch

T he rest of the morning was pretty normal except for the white noise in my brain stem that kept reminding me that things were really not normal.

At lunch I sat with Jax and Jason, and my friends Annika and James. Irene, the school cook, had solicited for fresh vegetables and scored about a million zucchinis from local gardens, so we'd been having zucchini in practically everything for days. Today it was zucchini tomato sauce over spaghetti.

"Sorry to hear about your dad," said Annika, methodically picking out the zucchini from her tomato sauce and placing it on the side of her tray.

"Yeah," said James, rhythmically stabbing his fork into each rejected piece of zucchini on Annika's plate and eating it.

Word traveled fast.

"Have you spoken to your mother since this morning?" asked Jax.

"Not yet," I said, twirling spaghetti around and around my fork.

"Here," said Annika, pulling her cell phone out of her bag, "use my phone."

She handed it to me.

This would probably be a good time to tell you about the totally unfair cell phone policy at Villa Rossini.

I am one of only about five sixteen-year-olds in America who still don't have their own cell phones.

My parents are against them. My mother doesn't think having that much electricity that close to your brain is good for the integrity of cell structure. She believes that cell phones cause brain cancer.

Recently I showed her a newspaper clipping that said that a new study had shown that cell phones do not cause brain cancer.

She took the article from me and read it over.

"You still can't have one," she said, handing the clipping back to me.

"Why?" I said. "They're safe. It says so right here."

"It would be interesting to see who funded this study," said my mother, "because you can be sure that in two weeks another group will rediscover that it does cause cancer."

"You don't care about me or my safety, do you?" I said. "I mean, what if I'm in an emergency or something?" I'm not sure what made me say that just then. I guess it had been on my mind, and her brushing me off seemed, I don't know, too cool to be maternal.

My mother regarded me soberly. "It is precisely because I care about you and your safety that I will *not* get you a cell phone," she said.

My father said they contribute to short-term memory loss because the speed-dial number storage system means you don't even have to remember phone numbers anymore and, more important to him, because they inhibit true communication between people. The last time I brought up the subject, he responded with this: "True communication is not being accessible by phone in the woods. True communication is being inaccessible by phone in the woods with someone you love."

He had a point.

Still, you could turn your cell phone *off* in the woods, right?

Anyway.

I took Annika's phone and with the other hand reached into my pocket and pulled out the piece of paper Mrs. P. had given me earlier. I hadn't wanted to make the call with Mrs. P.—but here, with my friends, it felt right.

My throat felt dry as I punched in the numbers. It barely rang before my mother picked up.

"Hello," she said.

"Hi, Mom."

"Angelina," she said. "I've been waiting to hear from you."

"Sorry, Mom," I said. I scanned the faces of my friends, who were all watching me intensely. James had even stopped eating. "How's Dad?"

"Your father is in intensive care," said my mother. Her voice sounded flat. "I'm spending the night here. I've arranged for you to spend the night at Liz's. I thought you might need some company."

Liz is my mother's best friend, and I've spent about 30 percent of my life with her. When I was four, I rode behind Liz on her horse Bill in the town's Fourth of July parade. My father had lifted me up to sit on Bill's big haunches. I wrapped my arms around Liz's waist. I still remember the smell of the suede vest she wore.

We paraded down Main Street right behind the Colonel, a World War II veteran in full dress uniform, and Mrs. Warren, his wife, wearing a red chiffon kerchief over her hair. They always rode in his '65 Mustang convertible in the parade, right in front of Sugar and the Dinettes, who marched in full waitress uniform and filled bystanders' coffee cups along the way.

"But Jax invited me to his house after school," I said.

"Okay," Mom said. "That's fine. When you're ready to leave, ask Jax to take you up to the house to let Mokey out, then see if he'll drive you down to Liz's. I am sure he won't mind."

"Okay," I said. Then there was a silence, like we were both waiting for the other to say something else.

I almost asked her how she was doing, when I heard a low moan in the background. Then my mother said, "Your father is awake. I'll see you in the morning," and broke the connection.

"Bye, Mom," I said into the void.

I shut the phone off and handed it back to Annika, who stowed it in her bag. I picked up my fork and pushed some food around on my plate. My friends all stared at me, but no one said anything.

"What?" I said.

"Well," said Annika tentatively, "how is he?"

"He's in intensive care," I said. "My mom's staying at the hospital tonight."

"People recover from stuff like this all the time," said Jason. "I mean, you always see stories about stuff like this on TV."

"And your dad's a strong guy," said Jax, putting his arm around my shoulders. "If anybody can make it through something like this, he can."

"Yeah," I said. "He is pretty strong for an old guy. Maybe you're right. He'll be okay."

"Just wait: He'll be slicing pizza just like always at the next Town Market Day," Jason said, flipping imaginary pizza dough into the air. "*Ciao! Ciao, bella!*"

We laughed.

Jason stood up and very dramatically continued to toss the imaginary pizza. The kids at other tables watched him and laughed too. He bowed and threw a kiss, and the kids started to applaud.

"Perhaps you are confused, Mr. Andrews," said Mr.

Crispi, who was on lunch duty. "This is lunch, not dinner theater."

"Yes, sir," Jason said, and sat down.

"Still," Mr. Crispi continued, "if you bring half the animation that you gave to this dramatic effort to the winter concert, our show can't help but be a success."

"Huh?" said Jason.

Mr. Crispi smiled and walked away.

"I think he meant you were entertaining," I said.

"Duh," said Annika.

"I mean I think he meant he wasn't really mad at you," I said.

"For now, that is," said Jax, picking up his tray. We picked up our trays too and followed him to the window.

I love my friends.

Logger Genes

I know I said this before, but I love going to the Tatros' house. Jax's great-grandfather Rosaire built it back at the beginning of the last century, and then Jax's grandfather bought it, and now Jax's father owns it. One of these days it will probably belong to Lucien, Jax's oldest brother and the one with the highest number of logger genes. About a month ago Lucien's wife, Denise, went back home to live with her mother and took their eighteen-month-old daughter, Raven, with her because Lucien was drinking too much. He quit, but she's waiting a little longer to see if it takes.

A little about the rest of Jax's family:

Allan, Jax's middle brother, worked in the woods when he was a teen, then studied accounting. He's the family CPA and he lives the bachelor lifestyle in Saint Albans, where he owns a small house. You never see him with the same girl twice.

Jax's youngest older brother, Sean, works in the woods and competes in pulling events at fairs all over the state. In case you don't know, a pulling event is a competition with teams of titanic horses pulling wooden sleds piled with half-ton cement blocks. The winner is the team that can pull the heaviest load over a line drawn in the dirt. And there's lots of consumption of the three basic pulling food groups: beer, jerky, and Little Debbie cupcakes.

Sean built a house up behind his dad's and keeps his big horses there. He's had a hard time holding on to girl-friends and, so far, one wife because he spends so much time with Charlie and Ned, his horses.

His last two horses were called Dan and Charlie, and the horses before that were called Dan and Ned. For a while he had a mare named Belle, but it must've really rattled him, because pretty soon he replaced her with another Charlie.

Anyway.

Sean was lounging against the doorjamb watching TV when we walked into the house. He grabbed Jax as we passed and put him in a headlock, then gave him noogies on his scalp. He's about six inches shorter than Jax, but he still thinks of himself as Jax's big brother.

"Hey!" he said to me, but he quickly changed his joking look. He put his large hand on my head and said in a somber voice, "Sorry."

"Thanks, Sean," I said.

"What's this?" Jax asked, pointing to the TV.

"Some Japanese dating show or something," said Sean. "Dad got this new dish. You can get channels from Japan."

Jax sat down next to his mother. I sank to the floor near Mrs. T.'s legs, and she reached down and patted my shoulder.

On-screen this Japanese woman with long blond curls—must have been a wig?—was sitting across a small table from a Japanese guy. She said something and then covered her mouth with her perfectly manicured hand and laughed. She had these long eyelashes and extreme foundation. Up in the left corner of the screen was an inset of this other guy wearing a baseball cap that said BEAUTIFICATION ENFORCEMENT AREA, and he was talking into a headset. It appeared that he was wired to the guy at the table. Up in the right corner was an inset of another girl, also speaking into a headset. Her hair was short and spiky, with red streaks.

"I think the little guys in the corners are the puppet masters," said Sean. "What do you think, Ma?"

Mrs. T. stood up.

"*Ils sont fous, ces Japonais*," she said.

"*Pazzo*, as my father would say," I said. Everyone looked at me. Silence fell. A split second later my brain registered what I'd said and I remembered where my father was, and I slapped my hand over my mouth.

Mrs. T. stood up and held out her hand to me.

"I am baking bread, Angelina," she said. "Join me." I reached up and took her hand, and when I stood, she put her arm around my shoulders and we walked into the kitchen.

A big blue ceramic bowl covered with a checkered dish towel sat on the counter. Mrs. T. and I washed our hands, then she slipped an apron over my head and tied it in back.

She sprinkled some flour on the countertop, then tipped the dough out of the bowl and divided it into two equal pieces. She handed one to me and showed me how to punch it down and knead the air out of it.

"Push it away, den fold it back at you, den push it away again," she said in her heavy French-Canadian accent.

"Use ze 'eel of ze 'and. Add ze flour if it is too sticky." She set the canister of flour between us.

I tried it, and it was very Zen, you know, very soothing. Push the dough away. Fold it, turn it, and push it away again. It kind of felt like I was pushing my mom and dad and their situation away from me every time I did it.

"*Bon*," she said. "Very good." She sprinkled a little flour on my piece of dough, then said, quite casually, "'Ow are you?"

And that's when I started to cry.

Tears fell on my dough, and Mrs. T. moved it out of the way. "It doesn't need more water or more salt!" she said. I just shook my head, and she wrapped her floury arms around me, and I sobbed into her shoulder. She is plump and she smells good: like sugar and butter and lemon zest. And she's young. *She's everything a mother should be,* I thought, and I hugged her back.

She talked to me in a soothing voice. She told me the story of her own father's stroke. She wasn't sixteen, like me, but it sounded awful just the same.

"Did he get better?" I asked.

Mrs. T. wiped my tears away with her thumbs. She looked at me, then looked away and said, "No, *chéri*. 'Ee did not." She sighed. "But you know, I tink it was better zat way. You 'ave to be strong to live wiz someone 'oo looks like someone you once knew but isn't really zat person anymore, you know?"

I nodded, but I didn't really understand what she meant.

Not yet.

Dinner

❧❀❧

"Jacques!" *Mrs. T. called after* we had shaped the loaves and covered them to let them rise for the second time.

Jacques is Jax's given name. Jacques Henri, if you can believe that. I started calling him Jax when I learned how to read and saw his name spelled out for the first time. Jax himself came up with the current spelling.

Now Mrs. T.'s about the only one who still calls Jax by his given name.

Jax came into the kitchen. Mrs. T. spoke to him in rapid French, and Jax collected plates and silverware and took them to the dining room to set the table.

There was a knock at the back door, the door opened, and Denise burst into the mudroom carrying Raven. She put the little girl down, and Raven ran into the kitchen.

"Mimi!" she shouted.

Her grandmother picked her up.

"They back yet?" asked Denise, slipping out of her shoes and coming into the kitchen in her bare feet.

"No," said Mrs. T.

Denise nodded, then took an apron off a hook on the wall and started working on a salad.

"Sorry to hear about your dad," she said to me. "Any news?"

"They have to watch him tonight," I said. "My mom's staying at the hospital overnight."

Mrs. T. gave the baby to me, and Raven settled into my lap.

"Where are you staying?" she asked. "You want to stay with us?"

"I'm covered, thanks," I told her.

Raven stood up in my lap and started playing with my hair.

Denise turned to her mother-in-law.

"I'm back," she said.

"I'm glad," said Mrs. T.

The back door opened, and Mr. T. ducked under the doorframe, filling the space in the small back room with the smell of the woods, gasoline, sweat, and cigarette smoke.

Mrs. T. helped him take off his logging boots, and he stepped into the kitchen in his dirty socks. He towered over Mrs. T. and had to bend down to kiss her on the cheek. He nodded at me, then turned on the water and started washing his hands. You could tell Mr. T. had been something of a Baldwin when he was younger. He has sharp blue eyes and long, dark lashes, and his hair is thick and wavy and gray.

The door opened again and Lucien stamped in. He's about the same size as Mr. T. and looks a lot like Mr. T. probably did when he was young. In other words, he's pretty cute.

"Denise!" he said when he saw her at the counter, and he smiled so big I thought his face would break. He stepped into the kitchen wearing his logging boots. He took one step, then pulled up short.

The two Mrs. T.'s stood side by side, arms folded across their chests, and glared at him—and I think it was the combined force of their glare that stopped Lucien dead in his tracks. Mrs. T. ruled her house with an iron hand. Denise had eleven brothers. Together they were fearless in their handling of men.

Lucien threw me a glance and smiled sheepishly, then

stepped back into the entryway to remove his muddy boots.

Jax came back into the kitchen, and Sean followed.

"Is Allan coming?" asked Mr. T.

"Ee'll be late," said Mrs. T. "'Ee is going to ze gym to work out."

"If he worked in the woods, he wouldn't have to join a frickin' gym for five hundred dollars a year to build muscles," said Mr. T.

"Allan is a poet," said Mrs. T.

"Yeah, well, I hope he's not one of them queers, too," said Mr. T., turning the water off. I saw Mrs. T. steal a glance at Jax, and he looked down at the floor.

Mr. T. hung the dishtowel on its hook, then crossed to the refrigerator.

When he saw Jax, he smiled and reached out and tousled his hair affectionately, then opened the refrigerator and took out a beer.

"I'll have one too, Pop," said Lucien, stepping back into the kitchen in his stocking feet. Mr. T. tossed him a can, and he caught it neatly.

Denise looked up from what she was doing and waited.

"Actually," he said, putting the can on the counter, "not now." He stepped up behind Denise, turned her, lifted her up, and gave her a big kiss. She wrapped her arms around his neck and kissed him back. Then he put her down, reached out, and lifted his daughter out of my lap. She sat like a queen on the massive muscle of his forearm and pulled his hair. He smiled.

"Let's eat," said Mrs. T.

Dinner at the Tatros' is always an experience for an only child like me. In the first place, at least three, sometimes as many as five, grown men are present. Even though 50 percent of the Tatro boys are married, they still show up at their mother's house for dinner pretty much every night.

I wonder if Mrs. T. ever dreams of a day when she won't have to prepare large quantities of food.

Then, of course, you've got Raven and Denise and sometimes, but not that often, Sean's two kids, Hayley and Janessa.

And occasionally Allan's latest girlfriend.

And, sometimes, me.

Mrs. T. and Jax and Denise and I brought out several huge bowls of food and set them on the dining room table. Mrs. T. had sliced the bread we made, and put it in a basket. She placed a pitcher of ice water in front of Lucien. His own personal pitcher of ice water, which no one else is allowed to drink from, I might add. It's this historic mother/son thing between Mrs. T. and her oldest son. I think she thought Lucien's wife might take over this task, but Denise says forget it. She says unless Lucien's legs are both broken, he can get his own frickin' water. No personal pitchers in her house.

You've got to love Denise.

We ate in silence for a while. I was really hungry. Apparently, despite what movies and novels would have you believe, catastrophic events don't make all people lose their appetites entirely.

I must've been eating pretty fast, because Mr. T. looked at me and said, "You're little, but you eat like a logger."

"I'm an accountant and *I* eat like that," said Allan, walking into the dining room. He kissed his mother and sat down, took a plate, and filled it.

Then it went like this:

Lucien: "Maybe Pop means you eat like a Tatro."

Mrs. T.: "I'm a Tatro and I don't eat like zat."

Sean: "You're not a true Tatro, Mom."

Denise: "Count your blessings."

Then she and Mrs. T. exchanged a knowing glance.

"It could be gender related," Denise continued.

"I'm not so sure," Jax said. "Look at Raven."

We all looked at Raven. She was hunched over the tray of her high chair, shoveling food into her mouth with both her spoon and her hand.

"Another theory shot to hell," said Denise.

And we all burst out laughing.

Even me.

I remember feeling like I was there and not there at the same time. Like I was myself but also as if I were floating above myself, watching everything I did—as if it were me, but not me. And the part of me that was floating above felt guilty and kind of amazed that I could be having a good time now, but the other part of me, the part that was laughing, just kept right on laughing.

And you know what? I think Dad would have liked to see me then.

Back to Active Service

❧❧

A fter dinner Jax said he'd drive me home to let Mokey out (it wasn't too late—I could catch him before an accident) and to pack, and then drop me at Liz's.

As we crunched over the gravel, Mrs. T.'s manic German shepherd, Sweetie, barked insanely at the end of her chain.

"She's scary," I said.

Jax winked at me. "That's her job."

We climbed into a red truck that had TATRO AND SONS LOGGING painted on the door. Jax started the engine and we drove off. As usual Jax extended his right arm along the back of the seat and pulled me close to him. I slid over, straddled the stick shift, and pretended I was his girlfriend. As usual.

I know, pathetic. But given the kind of day I'd had, I figured I deserved a little pathetic fantasy fix.

Getting back to my love for Jax: I've had a thing for him ever since first grade, when he was the only boy who would play mean Barbies with me. All the girls just wanted to play that the Barbies were nice and had boyfriends and dressed up and had their hair done and lived in a pink plastic house and drove a pink plastic car. But Jax and I made the Barbies sisters, and one had a boyfriend and the other didn't, and we insulted each other and picked on each other and then just always ended up in a big Barbie fistfight and slapfest. Sometimes heads rolled.

Jax liked to play dress-up, too, long after most little boys had left the runway-model phase behind. I remember how gorgeous he looked in that emerald green gown I had, wearing matching plastic mules with marabou-feather poufs on the toes, a matching glittery purse hanging elegantly from one wrist. He looked much better in it than I did.

I still wonder, when I come across cross-dressers: Is it fair that some boys get long, thick eyelashes and look better in girls' clothes than we do? I am consoled by the thought of the price they pay: having their genitalia hang outside their bodies, thus making them feel totally vulnerable and threatened at all times. I really shouldn't complain.

Anyway, I've never really kissed Jax, unless you count the time when we were pretending to be Laura and Manly from the Little House books. I had to kiss him good-bye as he left our home to bury our infant son in the family graveyard.

And I really don't count that kiss.

Now, even though I understand who he is and I accept it and all—well, for the most part—the tragic truth is that I still love him in *that* way, and that, to paraphrase Rhett Butler, is my misfortune. Although I realize that I am *so* not realistic about him, as much as I try, I just can't seem to change the way I feel about him.

My father once told me that the heart and mind can work at odds with each other. Often do, in fact.

"So which is better?" I asked him.

He tapped his lips with his fingertip for a while and studied me, then he said, "The heart, *cara mia*. Everyone has a mind, but not everyone has a heart."

I think about this all the time, and sometimes I think I finally understand it—and then there are times when I'm still not sure exactly what it means. I thought about asking him again someday, and that thought brought me back to the present.

I turned to Jax.

"Do you think my father will be okay?" I asked him.

Jax sat quietly behind the wheel of the truck for a moment, then sighed and said, "I don't know."

He turned onto the main road. I rested my head on Jax's buff shoulder, and I guess I must've fallen asleep, because the next thing I knew, we were stopped in my driveway.

I jerked awake.

"How long have I been asleep?" I asked.

"About fifteen minutes," he said.

"Sorry," I said. "I'm not great company tonight, huh?"

"I figured you needed the sleep," he said, and shrugged.

"Did I snore, or drool?"

"Just a little," said Jax.

"Really?" I asked, shuddering.

"No," said Jax, smiling his ever-charming smile. "Look, no worries, okay?"

I rubbed my eyes, opened the door, jumped down from the truck, and crunched across my moonlit driveway. In response Mokey started yapping furiously in his kennel. I hurried into the house to get him.

"Poor Mokey!" I cooed, opening the cage door. "Such a long time in your crate!"

Mokey was out the door of the house like a shot. He immediately peed on the lawn, then did a big poop. When Jax got down from the cab, Mokey almost ripped some muscles in his excitement to see him. Even though he sees him just about every day.

I left the two boys together and went inside. I had to pee pretty badly myself, but I went all the way upstairs to do it; I couldn't bring myself to use the downstairs bathroom.

Once I got to my room, I threw some stuff into my overnight bag: a T-shirt and boxers, a toothbrush, toothpaste, clean underwear and socks, and shampoo. On impulse I pulled Tiger, my stuffed raccoon, off my shelf of childhood keepsakes. "Tiger," I said, "you're being called back into active service."

I tucked him under my arm and looked around the room. My eyes lingered on the photograph of my father on Town Market Day, brandishing the pizza cutter, his eyes crinkled with mischief and mirth at a private joke he was enjoying with himself. I picked up the photo and stuffed it into my bag as well. Then I shut off the light and left.

Lez Nest

❧❦❧

Jax told me that Truman Capote once said in a book called *Answered Prayers* that there's nothing as cozy as a lez nest.

"Who's Truman Capote?" I asked.

"Truman Capote was a small gay writer with a hat and a whiny voice," he said, "and he came out early in the twentieth century, when it was still pretty unusual to come out."

If you ask me, Truman Capote was right about the nest.

And if there was ever a place on Earth that proved this, it is Liz's cabin in the woods. It's so cozy it's almost a joke.

Liz moved into it with her girlfriend Kelly, but then Kelly left her for a younger woman. I hated Kelly for a while. Now I just think she's an idiot. I mean, I can't understand why someone wouldn't want to be with Liz. But then, romantic relationships are always so screwy.

It was dark and the light in the cabin's kitchen window glowed, golden and warm. "Is there anything in the known universe as inviting as a lighted room in the dark?" I asked Jax as we pulled into Liz's driveway.

"A lighted room in the dark with someone who wants to see you waiting inside," said Jax with a little sigh.

I turned to look at him; he had his elbow on the steering wheel and was leaning his cheek on his fist, gazing at Liz's house.

He must've felt me looking at him, because he turned his head and gave me a sheepish smile.

I opened the truck door, slammed it shut, then walked around the truck to stand at Jax's window. He rolled it down and I kissed his cheek.

"Thanks," I said.

"Call if you need anything," Jax said. He leaned out and gave me a kiss on my cheek, then rolled up the window and backed out of the driveway.

I turned and walked down the stone steps to Liz's front door, opened it, and walked into her house.

"Put your stuff down, honey, and bring me a piece of

steel wool from the bag that's on the table, would you?" said Liz. The door to the cabinet under the sink was open, and her legs stretched along the floor in front of it, among the cleaning supplies and trash can that usually occupied the undersink zone.

Her cat Brezhnev was perched precariously on her hip, and he was washing his face.

I put my bag on one of the chairs, picked up the bag of steel wool, and handed a piece to her.

"Thanks, honey," she said.

I sat down on the floor beside her with my back against the cabinet. Brezhnev stretched, then jumped off of Liz and transferred himself to my lap. I stroked him, and he purred in response. I heard the sound of steel wool being pulled apart, then a few knocks and small grunts, and then, "Get through *that*, you mice!" Then Liz pulled her upper half out of the cabinet.

"I have just deployed my latest antimouse strategy," she said, repopulating the cabinet with the trash can and cleaning supplies. "Plugging mouse access points with steel wool."

She closed the cabinet door and scooted her butt back up against it so we were sitting side by side. "Mice can't chew through steel wool. Or so I was told by a loquacious exterminator."

Liz can't bring herself to kill the mice in her cabin just for being mice and doing what mice do: coming into houses in the fall and building nests and gathering food. Liz respects their amazing survival instincts. At the same time, she is tired of finding mouse poop on the kitchen counter and in her silverware drawer. She has a Havahart trap too—you know, the kind of trap that doesn't kill. She baits it every night with peanut butter, and in the morning she takes the caught mouse (there is *always* a mouse) to what she calls the West Hill Mouse Preserve and sets it free, miles from anyone else's house, to practice its amazing survival instincts in the wild.

I've often wondered if it's possible that the same mouse keeps finding its way back to Liz's for just the same reason I do: It's so welcoming.

"As long as they stay out of my kitchen," Liz said, "I think the mice and I can maintain a peaceful coexistence." Then she looked at me carefully. "You look tired, honey," she observed. "How are you holding up?"

In response I put my head down on her shoulder. She put her arm around me and kissed me lightly on the top of my head. It's something she's been doing all my life, but it felt especially good that night.

"I don't know," I said. "It's mostly totally surreal. Sometimes I feel really out of it, and other times things seem sorta normal."

"I guess in the grand scheme of things this *is* normal. Health, sickness. You know," Liz said.

"Yeah, but what about death?"

There. I'd said it.

"He's not dead," said Liz. "Hang in there, Angelina." She patted my leg, then stood up. "How about some tea?" she said. "Let's have chamomile. It's a calming herb."

She offered me her hand and pulled me to my feet.

"And let the other cat in, will you?" she said, grabbing the kettle and filling it at the sink. "I hear him scratching." She put the kettle on the stove and lit the burner.

I heard the scratching too and opened the front door. No cat. I crossed the room and opened the back door. No cat. The scratching continued. Liz looked puzzled, then suddenly got this *Eureka!* look on her face. She stepped across the kitchen and opened the door to the cabinet under the sink. Khrushchev emerged from the cabinet, but only halfway: His front paws were on the kitchen floor, his hindquarters remained under the sink. He looked around the room.

"Poised between dimensions," said Liz, shaking her head. "You can't rush into these transitions." She began slowly closing the cabinet door. When it was about a millimeter from Khrushchev's body, he casually licked one paw, then slipped out and made a break for the bedroom.

"Houston, we have reentry," said Liz, shutting the cabinet with a bang.

The kettle whistled and the phone rang at the same time. I chose the kettle.

That left the phone for Liz, who crossed the room and answered it.

"Nicola. Hello," Liz said into the receiver. She listened for a minute, then said, "Hmmm. That's rough. How are you holding up?" Another pause. "Okay. Yep. See you tomorrow. Keep breathing." She handed the phone to me. "It's your mom," she said. I took the phone from Liz and handed her the kettle.

"How's Dad?" I asked.

"The same," said my mother.

"Is that all you're going to tell me?" I said angrily.

"Don't I deserve a little more information than just 'the same'?"

I heard my mother sigh. "Angelina, please," she said. "I'm going through this too."

"Yeah, but you're with him," I said.

There was a pregnant pause, then my mom said, "Look, Angelina, I'm—"

I didn't let her finish. I know that wasn't fair, but at that point being fair was not one of my top priorities. I felt slighted: gypped out of news about my dad.

"See you tomorrow, then," I said, and I hung up without saying good-bye. Maybe I just needed some space.

"Let's go feed the horses," said Liz. She had poured hot water into two thermal mugs and screwed their covers on. She handed one to me and kept one for herself.

She pulled on her barn boots and an old barn coat, jammed a Tatro and Sons Logging cap on her head, took two carrots from a big bag by the door, and walked outside. I took two carrots of my own, then followed her out the front door and into the night.

We walked across the yard and slipped under the fence wire. The air was fresh and crisp, and the stars glittered against the inky sky. I thought of my father and me on

Midnight Rock, a great half-buried glacial erratic boulder in our yard where my father and I spent many nights lying on our backs and looking at the stars. I started crying. Quietly.

I think Liz knew I was crying, but she had the sense not to let me know she knew, and I didn't let her know I knew she knew. I wiped a couple of tears from my cheeks, then wiped my nose on my sleeve.

Liz stopped. I stopped beside her. We waited.

I felt them before I heard them. Their heavy footsteps beat the earth. Soon I heard a horse blow quietly, then saw a pair of eyes shining in the moonlight, and Bill and Hillary slowly materialized out of the darkness and stopped. They stood before us, huge heads stretched forward, nostrils sniffing us expectantly.

Bill and Hillary were big and warm, and their breath was sweet in my face. I put my arms around Hillary's broad neck and hugged her. She tolerated this for a while, until Liz offered Bill a carrot. When he crunched it between his teeth, Hillary pulled her head away and waited for hers.

"You knew you'd get one, didn't you?" I said, breaking off a piece and offering it to her on the palm of my hand. She whisked it up with her soft lips and crunched.

When we had fed them all the carrots we had, Liz and I went into the barn, took some hay, and put it into piles around the pasture.

Bill chose a pile and began to eat. Hillary sniffed the other two piles and found them wanting, so she walked up to Bill, ears pinned back, and nipped him in the rump. He walked patiently to another pile and began to eat there. I could swear I heard him sigh.

We sipped our tea and listened to them chewing for a while.

"A horse makes hay sound so delicious," said Liz. "I always want to try some whenever I hear it."

I pulled a piece of hay out of her hat and handed it to her.

"Chow down, girl," I said. "You want ketchup with that?"

She bit off a piece and chewed. And chewed. And chewed.

"It's good for you. Lots of fiber," she said, and draping her arm across my shoulders, she chewed some more.

That night, tucked into the spare bedroom in Liz's little cabin, I snuggled with Tiger and dreamed about my father. We were riding horses together. Suddenly he turned to me and smiled. "*Ti voglio bene*," and turned and urged his horse on, his bathrobe flying out behind him. They ran faster and faster down a long dirt road, until they reached the vanishing point. I tried to follow, but my horse wouldn't go. I called and called after them, but they didn't come back. We stood under a tree, and the leaves kept hitting my face. They were wet and rough, and when I woke up, Brezhnev was licking the tears off the side of my nose.

A Surprising Thing About Evolution

❧❀❧

The next day was pretty normal. I got on the bus at Liz's house. (By now I don't have to tell you that Laila knew where I was staying, do I?) In math Annika got in trouble for writing her name on the collar of James's shirt in green dry-erase marker. We had a grammar quiz in English that I had totally forgotten about, and in Web Management we unveiled the new virtual tour we'd designed for the BHS website.

In chorus I kept catching Celeste glaring at me when she thought I wasn't looking.

Have I mentioned that we're doing an Andrew Lloyd Webber revue for our winter concert? We'll be singing songs from all of his shows, including *Phantom of the Opera*, *Cats*, *Jesus Christ Superstar*, and, my personal favorite, *Evita*. Celeste has the big finale, "Don't Cry for Me, Argentina."

My father was totally psyched about our program choice. On the first day of rehearsals he showed up at the school carrying his entire collection of Webber CDs and thrust them at Mr. C.

"This is northern Vermont," he said. "You need all the help you can get." Then he sat at the back of the room and listened to the whole rehearsal, fingers laced behind his head, smiling and nodding in time with the music.

At the end of rehearsal he said, "Mr. C., if I were you, I'd write a letter to Andrew Lloyd Webber and invite him to this unusual display of his genius."

"Think he'd come?" asked Mr. C.

"He'd be a fool not to," said my father, "and since I could never feel such passion for the music of a fool, he must not be a fool!"

Then he burst into our leitmotif, "Don't cry for me, Angelina," and threw his arm over my shoulder, and we left.

This afternoon the room seemed to echo with his absence.

We had just finished our rendition of "Memory," one of the corniest yet most powerful songs ever written, and it was time for the grand finale. Celeste stepped forward.

Mr. C. tossed his Looney Tunes tie over his shoulder and hit the opening chord on the piano, and Celeste opened her mouth and sang.

In one of the more surprising developments in the evolution of modern humankind, Celeste Larivee has a voice like an angel. And even though I loathe and despise her, I would walk barefoot through red-hot coals to hear her sing. Well, okay, maybe not barefoot over red-hot coals, but barefoot over pea stone for sure.

We all just stood there transfixed as she belted out *Evita*'s most famous song. When she finished, I just stared, with tears in my eyes. She caught me looking, and for once she didn't glare or sneer. Her face looked softer, somehow, and sweet.

Okay. Semisweet. But not hateful.

So I smiled at her.

Big mistake. Her whole face immediately hardened and cooled. "What are you lookin' at?" she said, really challenging me.

"That was awesome," I said, still too touched by her voice and the association with my father to react in my usual hostile manner.

I guess I took Celeste completely by surprise, because

she opened her mouth to make a crack, then just closed it, kind of like a goldfish. She looked quickly away, then sat back down in her seat.

Mr. C. jumped up and called for our attention.

"Okay, singers," he said. "That was a decent run-through. Keep listening to your practice tapes, and I'll see you next week, same time, same station."

Celeste jumped down off the platform and slammed right into Jax, deliberately elbowing him in the ribs.

"Ooooooofff!" said Jax.

"Hey!" I said, turning to Celeste. "Watch where you're going."

Celeste turned on me.

"Listen, sister," she said. "Just because your father had a catastrophic accident doesn't mean I have to stop bothering *him*." She gave Jax the stink eye.

That was more than enough to snap me out of my little Celeste-love moment. I hauled back to slug her, when Jax grabbed my arm and stopped me.

"Forget it!" he said to me.

"It's too bad you've got the voice of Ariel trapped in the body of Ursula," I said.

I think I hurt her with that. I mean, she flinched and

looked down at the floor, then turned and walked out.

"That was harsh, Ange," said Jax as we walked to the parking lot. "As Granny Nancy says, make peace, not war." He gave me the peace sign.

"You don't mean that." I said.

"Look," he said, "I used to get defensive all the time. But then one day, when I was working in the woods with Lucien and my dad, something happened. You know Geoff, the guy who comes up from NYC every summer? Owns the old sugarhouse on the Montgomery Mountain Road and walks in the woods with his partner, Everett, and their whippet, Kate?"

I nodded. I knew whom he meant.

"Well, they walk by the lot we're cutting. Maybe they were holding hands. I don't remember. And Lucien waits until they're not quite out of earshot, then says, just loud enough for them to hear, 'We're taking back Vermont, faggots!'

"Well, I jumped him. Lucien, I mean. And I was hauling back to punch him for the second time when my father grabbed my arms and pinned them behind my back. No one said anything, but at that moment I think we all understood something."

"But your dad made a remark about queers just last night," I said.

Jax nodded. We got in his truck.

"We have never spoken about it again," he said. "About the incident. About the reality that I'm gay. And the little comments? I guess it's his way of making it very clear that his position on queerness has not changed, without challenging me directly. It's a strictly 'don't ask, don't tell' situation. Of course, the little comments do sting. But they're better, I think, than what might happen if I just came out to him."

He sighed. "Anyway, it's nothing a little Andrew Lloyd Webber can't cure."

He popped our practice tape into the tape player, and we belted out Webber songs together the rest of the way home.

A Tough Old Bastard

❧❦❧

When *I walked into the kitchen,* my mother was sitting at the table. She looked terrible; dark, bruise-like circles under her eyes, her hair spiky on one side and matted on the other. Her clothing looked like she had slept in it—which, I quickly realized, she had. There was a cup of coffee in front of her, but it looked like she hadn't touched it.

She massaged her brow with the fingers of her left hand and absently stroked Mokey with the other. Mokey lay quietly on her thighs, breathing softly, his eyes closed. I had never seen him so calm. When I came in, he opened his eyes, ID'd me, then shut them again.

"Mom?" I said.

She raised her head slowly, as if she had been in a trance. It took a few seconds for her eyes to focus. Then she nodded, confirming that she was, in fact, my mother.

I sat down opposite her in my father's chair. She noticed, looked as if she was about to say something, then changed her mind and sighed instead.

"How's Dad?" I asked.

My mother shook her head.

"He's *dead*?" I asked, bolting up out of my chair. It tipped over and landed with a crash. Mokey was off her lap in an instant, barking insanely at the offending piece of furniture.

"No," she said, and she sounded almost mad. "Worse than that. He's paralyzed. His whole right side. Can't speak. Can't even swallow by himself." She looked into her coffee cup, somber and maybe a little lost.

"But he's still alive," I said, finding my breath again. "That's good, right?"

My mother looked me straight in the eyes, put her hands on each of my cheeks, and pulled my face down to hers. She gave me a kiss, and I could smell the hospital on her, and sweat, and under that, a hint of her perfume: Kenzo.

"We'll just have to wait and see, won't we?" she said gently.

And then my mother started to cry. She pulled herself away from me, sat down, and covered her face with her hands. Unless you know my mother, you can't possibly understand the shock factor. I had never seen my mother cry before. That's so not something my mother does. I wasn't sure what I felt. I felt weird, sure, but I also felt scared, because if she was crying, then things had to be *really* bad.

But wasn't he alive? That was good—right?

I grabbed a handful of tissues from the box on the counter and held them out to my mother. It took her a minute to notice, then she looked up at me and smiled. She wiped her hand on her pants, took the tissues from me, dried her eyes, and gave her nose a blow.

"If he's alive, why are you crying?" I asked.

"Sit down, my darling," she said, patting the seat of the chair beside her, "and let me tell you about my past twenty-four hours. Then you can tell me about yours. Or wait—would you like to tell me about yours first? I know I could use a good diversion about now."

"Okay," I said. "Well. Today was better than yesterday. Yesterday I had a fight with Celeste and punched her and got sent to the principal's office. Today I had a fight with

Celeste but I didn't punch her. Also, on the plus side, I'm not doing drugs and I'm not pregnant. I mean, not today."

My mother laughed.

"Thank you for that," she said, patting me on the cheek. "You remind me of your father right now: He can always lighten up a situation."

We both sat quietly for a moment. Then my mother licked her lips and bit her lower one.

"Yes," she said. "Well."

Then she breathed in through her nose and exhaled through her mouth and said, "My turn."

I waited.

"When we first got to the hospital," she said, "they hooked your father up to a bunch of machines. He had tubes in his arm, tubes up his nose—even a tube up his penis."

Whoa.

Did I really want to hear this?

"His heart was hooked up electronically to a monitor. His brain waves were being broadcast on a TV screen. *Beep. Beep. Beep.*" She gave a short, bitter laugh. "He was wired. Wired for bloody sound."

She stopped for a minute and looked at her cup.

"Can I get you some fresh coffee, Mom?" I reached for the cup. My mother shook her head, pulled the cup away from me, and continued.

"I sat beside him," she said, "and held his hand. I could see the panic in his eyes. They darted from the tubes in his arm to the monitors on the wall to me and then back to the tubes again. I stroked his hair and he closed his eyes. Then, I don't know, I must have fallen asleep. Next thing I knew, alarms were going off. Loud. I woke with a start. My clothes were wet, and your father's tubes were flapping, hanging, dripping on the floor, on my lap. He was no longer holding my hand. I don't even think he was breathing." She looked at me, then continued in a voice now sort of tinged with admiration and awe. "He had ripped his ruddy tubes out! He can only use his left hand—and he used that!" She smiled and shook her head. "The tough old bastard!"

"He ripped out his tubes?" I asked. "But he could have died!"

"I know," said my mother, and she fixed me with a steady gaze.

Suddenly I was hit hard with the full impact of what this meant. "Oh."

"Exactly," she said.

"The nurses came rushing in as soon as the alarms went off," she said, "and hooked him back up again. When I looked into his eyes again, I saw a look of the purest defeat. Then they restrained his left hand and gave him something to make him sleep."

My mother stood up and took her cup to the sink. She poured out her coffee and rinsed the mug.

"Angelina," she whispered without turning from the sink, "I confess to you that I almost pulled those tubes back out myself."

Time out.

Did my mother just confess to almost killing my father?

"What?" I shouted.

My mother turned and looked at me. I saw pain in her eyes, and then I saw them harden. "You can't possibly understand," she said. "You're too young."

"I understand perfectly," I said. "You thought about killing my father!"

"It's more complicated than that, Angelina," said my mother wearily.

We had done a debate on the right to die in Current

Events class, and I had been on the pro side. We'd addressed all the big questions: What is life? What is death with dignity? Who controls your death? But it was *way* different when you were talking about it in terms of how these questions affected your own father.

My mother put the mug into the dish drain and dried her hands on the dish towel. She hung her head over the sink, and I knew she was crying again.

"Anyway, you win," I said.

"Beg pardon?" asked my mother thickly.

"You win," I said again. "Your day was way worse than mine."

My mother sniffed hard, then wiped her cheeks with the heels of her hands.

"Is there a prize?" she asked.

I scooped Mokey up from the floor. "Yes," I said, handing him to her. "You win this mostly housebroken dog."

"Lovely," said my mother, taking Mokey from me. He immediately began licking the tears from her face. "But tell me, what kind of day do you have to have to win a *totally* housebroken dog?"

We laughed, and my mother stood on her toes and kissed me on the forehead.

"Well, I've got to get back to the hospital," she said, regaining her composure. "I only came back to shower and pack up some clean clothes. Your sister should be here in a few hours."

She put Mokey down and turned to leave.

I guess it made sense that my sister was coming—but it didn't have me jumping for joy.

"When can I see him?" I asked, trying to take my mind off Francesca.

"Give me tonight, Angelina," she said. "Then we can talk about it."

"When?" I asked.

"Soon," she said. "Please don't pester me. Your father needs me."

She headed for the hall.

"Maybe he needs me, too," I said softly.

But she didn't hear me. She had already started climbing the stairs.

A Good Rule of Thumb When You're Eavesdropping

❧

When I was a little kid, I was really confused about exactly how Anthony was related to me. Technically, he is my nephew, but I referred to him as my son-in-law. He's actually my father's grandson, even though I am only six months older than he is. This set up quite a competitive dynamic between my sister and my mother, which did not help me and my sister develop a warm, fuzzy relationship with each other. My mom and my sister competed over first teeth (him), first steps (him), first words (me), first pee in the toilet (me again), height, weight, grades, sports, shoe size, and, to top it all off, my father's attention.

When we were three (actually, I was three and a half), my father picked up Anthony and kissed him, and I bit Anthony on the leg. When we were five, my father pulled me into his lap, and Anthony marched over and pushed me off. Hard.

You don't have to be a psychiatrist to see what this was all about.

When we were ten, my father and I had this big blowup over whether we should invite Anthony to lie on Midnight Rock with us and watch the Perseid meteor shower.

I didn't want him to.

No surprise there.

My father thought I should share.

"Midnight Rock is our rock!" I said. "It's our tradition."

"Is our tradition so small that we can't invite someone else in once in a while?" he asked me.

"I don't want him to," I said. I don't remember if I stamped my foot, but I'm pretty sure I folded my arms across my chest and scowled.

We were standing outside by Midnight Rock at the time. Anthony stood on the threshold of the doorway, a silhouette against the light in the mudroom behind him. My father looked at me, then turned and crossed the driveway. He spoke quietly to Anthony; it reached me as a low murmur, rising and falling in volume, sounds without meanings. Then Anthony disappeared into the house.

My father came back and lay down beside me. We looked up into deep space. Nothing was happening yet. Pretty soon I heard footsteps on the gravel. I sat up and saw Anthony carrying a lawn chair. He walked right toward us.

"Dad!" I whispered. "I told you I didn't want him to sit with us. It's our rock."

"But it's not our sky, Angelina," said my father.

Without giving me a glance, Anthony opened the lawn chair and placed it on the grass beside Midnight Rock. He sat down. I'm not sure, but I think I saw my father catch Anthony's eye, then wink and nod at him before he lay back down beside me, and we all watched the meteors streak across the heavens.

Some part of me has always loved Anthony for doing that.

Francesca feels that Anthony hasn't gotten the attention a first—and only—grandchild should get from a grandfather, since that grandfather also has a daughter who could be his granddaughter.

My sister's not a bad person. She works for the Pueblo Indians out in New Mexico using her legal power for the forces of good. As a megalawyer, she just hates being in a power-down position, and when it comes to Anthony and me, that's just where she thinks she is.

Plus, she's never really forgiven my father for divorcing her mother and marrying someone else—someone only sixteen years older than she is. Someone who really took her father away emotionally and then had a child in addition.

Talk about power-down.

All this is to say that I awaited my sister's arrival with mixed feelings.

I spent some time that afternoon surfing the Internet for info on strokes. Do you know there are almost five million sites with references to strokes? Here are just a few of the things I found out:

- The major causes of stroke are high blood pressure and stress.
- Even though the risk of stroke increases with age, a stroke can happen to anyone at any time—even young people. Remember Almanzo "Manly" Wilder? Laura's husband in the Little House books? Well, he had a stroke when he was in his thirties.
- People whose strokes occur in the left hemisphere of the brain become paralyzed on their right sides, and they can become

aphasic. That means they lose some or all of their ability to
speak and process language.
- Some people recover completely; some people don't recover at all.
  There is a rock band called the Strokes (their music is only okay,
  so say three reviewers).

The phone rang while I was on the computer. It was
Annika.

"What are you doing?" she asked.

"Reading about strokes and waiting for my sister," I
said. "Did you know that a stroke is also known as a brain
attack?"

"When's your sister coming?" she asked.

"Don't know. Soon," I said. "Did you know that sometimes if a stroke affects your speech center, you start speaking the language you learned most recently, not the one
you learned first?"

"You mean, if I had a stroke, I'd suddenly start talking
Spanish?" she said.

"Pretty scary," I said. "You only got a C minus in
Spanish on your last report card."

"*Muy malo*," she said.

"Did you know that people who suffer a stroke in the

right hemisphere of their brains often act impulsively, while people who suffer a stroke in the left hemisphere often become cautious?"

"I'm impulsive, and I haven't even had a stroke yet," she said.

"How do you know?" I said. "Did you know that TIAs, little tiny strokes, can occur without you even knowing it?"

"Uh-huh. Angelina?" she said. "Call me if you need me."

We hung up. I printed out the information, then went downstairs.

While I was making myself a snack of peanut butter on rice cakes, I heard a car pull into the driveway. I guess I was tenser than I thought, because I pressed too hard with the knife, and a piece of rice cake broke off and fell to the floor, where Mokey inhaled it. You have to maintain a light touch with rice cakes and peanut butter, or they just crumble to pieces in your hands.

I took a careful bite of my delicate snack as my sister walked in the door. She is short and stocky—like my dad—with thick, curly black hair that she wears Gina Lollobrigida style. There are not many twenty-first-century sixteen-year-olds who know who Gina Lollobrigida is—but there are not many twenty-first-century sixteen-year-olds who have a sixty-nine-year-old father from Italy. Gina Lollobrigida is a steamy Italian actress from the twentieth century. Francesca's eyebrows are black and slant up at the outer edges like bird wings. Her eyelashes are dark velvet fringes around her eyes. And her lips are red without lipstick.

In short, she's a babe.

"You shouldn't let that dog eat peanut butter," she said by way of greeting, putting her bag down on the floor. "He's already too fat."

Mokey ran right over to greet Francesca even though she had just dissed him big-time.

"Hello to you too, Francesca," I said.

My sister sighed.

So did I.

"Want some tea?" I asked. "Let's have chamomile. It's a calming herb."

My sister sat down with another big sigh. I poured some water into two mugs, added tea bags, and nuked them. When the tea was ready, I gave one mug to my sister and sat down at the table with my own.

"So what's going on?" she asked. "I mean with Dad?"

"Dad's paralyzed, and he can't talk," I said. "He pulled

his tubes out last night, so they had to restrain him."

"Does he have a living will?" she asked.

"I don't know," I said.

"He should," she said, and reached into her bag, pulled out a pen and notepad, and made a note.

"Dad doesn't need a living will yet," I said to Francesca. "It isn't like he's being kept alive by those tubes or anything."

Francesca studied my face. I don't know what she saw there, but when she spoke, it was in a softer-than-usual voice, "Are you sure?"

Then she closed her notepad and clicked her pen shut.

"What caused all this, anyway?" Francesca asked in her normal tone, putting the things back in her bag. "How has stuff been at home? Was there a lot of stress here?"

"Um, sorry, but are you trying to blame us?" I asked.

"Teenagers *always* cause stress," she said, more to herself than to me. "God knows Anthony gives *me* high blood pressure with his secretiveness and hostility and rebellious defiance. It's a wonder *I* didn't have a stroke." She gave a little self-conscious laugh and looked at me to see if I was smiling.

I wasn't.

"It's not my fault," I said, trying not to cry. "Don't try to blame me."

I stood up. Mokey, who had been curled up in a corner, got to his feet and stood by me.

"No one's blaming you, really," said my sister, blaming me with the tone of her voice. "It's just that he's old to have a young child like you. To be with a teenager every day at his age and, on top of that, to have such a young wife making sexual demands—it all puts quite a strain on him, I'm sure."

"*It's not our fault!*" I shouted again, then I threw my tea at her.

It seemed like a good idea at the time.

A wave of tea caught her in the chest. Fortunately, it wasn't hot anymore. Not really. But my sister jumped up and glared at me. Then she smiled, a superior smile, as if I had just proved her point.

Which I guess I had.

"I can't help thinking that if he hadn't divorced my mother, he might not have had a stroke," she continued, twisting the knife. She took a napkin off the counter and started blotting her blouse.

It is undoubtedly this calm under pressure that makes her such a force in the courtroom.

But you know what? This wasn't a courtroom.

Enough.

"No," I said, low and mean. "You two would have given him a heart attack instead."

We stared at each other resentfully.

The phone rang. Francesca waited to see if I would get it. Instead I turned and walked out of the kitchen and went up to my room. Mokey followed me.

I heard Francesca's footsteps as she crossed the kitchen. When I got to my room, I reached for my phone and, listening carefully, lifted it at the exact same moment that she answered. Covering the mouthpiece, I pressed the phone to my ear.

"Hello?" said my sister.

"Francesca," said my mother's voice.

"Hello," Francesca said again, but this time with an icy edge. My sister has a thing about using my mother's name. She doesn't. "How's my father?" my sister demanded.

"Well, he's sleeping now." My mother sounded weary. "But it's not good, Francesca. It's not good at all. He still can't swallow by himself. And he still can't speak. . . ." My mother let that statement hang in the air, and the enormity of its implication filled the silence completely—

heavy and oppressive. My mother continued, her voice as tight as wire, "He can only use his left arm. He used it to pull out his tubes, so they restrained him."

"Angelina told me," my sister said. "I'm going to draw up a living will for him. When can I see him?"

I waited to see if my mother would react to the living will thing too, but she just said, "I was thinking you could come down tomorrow and bring Angelina."

"Is that a good idea?" my sister asked. "I mean, bringing Angelina. She's still pretty young—she might not be able to handle it. I left Anthony home for just that reason."

He's my father too. I thought it; I didn't say it. A good rule of thumb when you're eavesdropping is not to speak.

"She can handle it." My mother's voice was firm and no-nonsense. "He's her father too."

Yeah!

My mother gave my sister the particulars: floor, room number, etc. Then she said, "Put Angelina on."

At that moment a raccoon appeared in the tree outside my window, and Mokey went nuts barking. I pressed my hand into the mouthpiece, but it didn't work.

"I think she's already on," said my sister.

"Hi, Mom," I said sheepishly.

"Have you been listening this whole time, Angelina?"

"Yes."

"Rather sneaky of you," she said.

"Yes," I said. Another good rule of thumb when you're eavesdropping: If you're caught, go quietly. "So I can come and see Dad tomorrow, then?"

"Yes, but prepare yourself, Angelina," said my mother. "Your father is in a bad way. He is weak and helpless and . . ."

That's when it hit me.

Reality.

And I didn't want to go there.

I didn't want to talk about my father. And I definitely didn't want to talk to my mother about how bad my father was. Maybe Francesca was right; maybe I was too young to handle it.

The goddess of telephone conversations must have been eavesdropping on her extension, because just then the beep of call-waiting sounded, and it was like music to my ear.

"Someone is trying to get through, Mom," I said. "I'll see you tomorrow."

"You can't run away from this, Angelina," said my mother.

But I could try.

"Bye," I said, and clicked the caller through. "Hello?"

"Hello, Angelina?" said a voice. "It's me. Anthony."

"Hi, Anthony," I said.

"How's Grandpa?" he asked.

"Pretty bad," I said. "He's paralyzed and he can't talk. And he has a tube up his wee-wee," I added as an after-thought.

"Did you say 'his wee-wee'?" Anthony asked.

"I did," I said, and we both snickered.

"It's really not funny," said Anthony.

"Yeah," I said. "I mean, no."

But we both laughed anyway.

"Do you want to talk to your mom?" I asked once I had gotten more or less back in control.

"No," he said.

And that started us off again.

"Are you sure you don't want to speak to her?" I asked.

"Well, all right," he said. "I'll talk to her."

"Hold on," I said. "Hey—thanks for calling, Anthony. I needed that laugh."

I shouted for my sister, and when I heard her pick up downstairs, I hung up.

* * *

Later that night I wandered into my mother and father's room and looked around. Except for some clothes that my mother had left on the bed when she changed, it looked pretty normal. My dad's slacks still hung over the back of his chair. His reading glasses were folded on the top book of a stack of books on his night table. A book lay open beside the stack. It was Dante, in Italian.

Photographs in frames stood on the top of his dresser. There was one of me and him when I was about eight, and another of him and Francesca when she was about eight. Though I had seen it all my life, I picked it up and studied it. The man in it was young. His hair was black, and he had no beard. He was wearing aviator sunglasses, smiling and squatting. My sister stood between his knees, one arm flung around his neck.

He was my father, and he was her father.

As if on cue, I felt an arm fall across my shoulder. Francesca. "I remember the day that picture was taken," she said. "I was angry because he wouldn't let me have an Atari. All my friends had one. He claimed video games ruined your mind."

"You know," I said, "that's the same argument he uses against cell phones!"

I put the photo back on the dresser and picked up the one of him and me. Francesca took it from me.

"He's still a good-looking guy," said Francesca.

"Yep," I said.

And then my sister turned to me.

"I'm scared," she whispered. "I don't want my father—our father—to die."

"Neither do I," I said.

My sister hugged me then, and at first it was sort of nice. Then it became only okay because she held on to me just a little longer than I felt was truly necessary, so I pulled away and said, "Let me help you with your suitcase."

I carried her suitcase to the spare room, said good night, and slipped out quickly just in case she had any ideas about hugging me again. Then I brushed my teeth and went to bed.

And even though it was only nine o'clock, I fell into a deep and dreamless sleep.

The Chaos Theory

✦❦✦

W hen *I was four,* my parents took me on a trip to Italy to visit my uncle Giancarlo. I don't remember much about the trip except that it was hot and I splashed in the fountain in the piazza with my small cousins, my uncle's grandchildren, who were roughly my age and who spoke no English. My uncle teased my father about me, saying how everyone must mistake my dad for my grandfather, but I could tell he was proud of his baby brother's virility. I am told that I was very good and that I impressed everyone by eating calamari with gusto.

By the time we left, I was saying *"Arrivederci!"* like a true paisano. There is a photo of us sitting at a table at an outdoor cafe. Dad is holding me and looking at me, and I can see how proud he is. My mother is sitting in the background, looking at my father and me with an unreadable expression on her face.

Perhaps it was the way my mother looked sitting by my father's bedside that triggered this memory, I don't know—but it's the first thing I thought when I stepped into his hospital room that next day. My sister had dropped me at the main entrance and had gone to find a parking spot, so I went in alone.

My father lay on the bed, tubes coming out of him in all directions from all body sites: those with and without natural access points. His face was slack, his hair was going haywire and looked a bit stained, a bit dirty, and gray stubble dotted his cheeks. His eyes were closed.

In other words, he looked ancient.

His blanket was disarranged and his hospital gown was hiked up, exposing his penis. My father has never been a modest man, but this was involuntary exposure—and he seemed so pathetic. I looked away, totally embarrassed and more than just a little weirded out.

I don't know what I'd expected—but it sure wasn't this old man lying in a bed with his weenie hanging out. I didn't know what to do or how to act.

My mother, suddenly noticing all this, stood up and rearranged his covers.

"You're flashing there, Andrea," she said, and laughed.

It was, I had to admit, a pretty cool reaction to the situation, and I remembered what my father had said about loyalty.

She patted the bed beside my father.

"Come sit, Angelina," she said, "so your father can see you. Look who's here, Andrea."

He opened his eyes. Left first, then slowly, like an afterthought, his right.

I hesitated, then strode purposefully to the bedside and looked down at my father's face. If I'd thought the glimpse I'd had of his wee-wee was upsetting, it was nothing compared with the discomfort level I reached seeing scum at the corners of his mouth and in the corners of his eyes.

Funny, isn't it? You'd think seeing your father's private parts would be much more of a downer than scum in his eyes, but it wasn't. My father was always so meticulous about his hygiene, so this sign of his own helplessness made me feel a little sick. But I forced myself to look at him.

"Hi, Daddy," I said. "How are you?" and then I caught myself. "Stupid question, huh?"

He let go of my mother's hand and reached out for mine.

I hesitated.

"Take his hand, Angelina," said my mother. "He isn't contagious."

I took his hand. It was warm and solid, and that made me want to kiss it, so I did—and he brought my hand to his lips, tears in his eyes, and suddenly it was all okay. I sat down on the edge of his bed and exhaled and inhaled deeply. I guess I'd been holding my breath, because it seemed as if that was the first breath I'd taken since I came into the room.

That's when I noticed the restraint tied to the head-board.

My father saw my glance.

"Ho ho," he said.

I looked at him.

"What?" I said.

He looked at my mother. He took his hand from mine and gestured at the restraint.

"He wants me to tell you that they tie him up at night so he won't pull out his tubes anymore," said my mother. "At the moment he seems able to make only one sound: 'ho.'"

I was totally not prepared for this. I caught myself

wondering if Francesca had been right after all about me not being ready.

I turned to my father.

"Ho," he said softly, then smiled and raised his left eyebrow as if he was making fun of himself, and I almost smiled; my father was still feisty even though he couldn't really speak and only had the use of one hand.

My mother plucked a tissue from the box on his bedside table, dipped it into his water glass, and wiped my father's mouth and the corners of his eyes.

"You need your morning facial, pet," she said.

I looked down, kind of embarrassed, like I should have done that or something. But I was ripped out of the thought by a shrill scream.

Francesca was standing in the doorway with her hand over her heart.

"Oh, my God! Daddy!" she spewed. "What's going to happen now?" and then she burst into tears.

My mother rolled her eyes.

My father shut his eyes.

I covered my eyes with my hand. Unfortunately, when I uncovered them, Francesca was still there.

And so were my father's tubes.

Later That Same Day ...

Before *we left the hospital,* my mother, sister, and I went down to the cafeteria to have something to drink and talk.

"Okay. So what's the plan?" asked Francesca after we had carried our drinks to a small table and sat down.

"Do we need a plan?" I asked.

Francesca put her hand on my shoulder and looked at me.

"Yes," she said.

My mother took a deep breath. "The plan, as I see it," she said, "is to watch him for the next few days, then transfer him to rehab, then discharge him to a convalescent facility, and then transfer him home."

"So they think he's going to recover?" I asked. My heart was hammering—I really hoped this was true.

"We don't know that, Angelina," said my mother.

"But you just said he's going to rehab and coming home," I said. "That means they thing he's going to live."

"They think he's going to *live*, Angelina," said my mother. "They said nothing about recovering."

"It's distinctions like these that make malpractice suits and right-to-die issues so difficult to define," said Francesca.

The picture of my father ripping out his tubes popped into my head. My mother's words about how complicated it all was echoed in my brain.

My mother looked at her watch, then stood up.

"I want to get back upstairs," she said.

We stood too. My mother reached out her arms and hugged me, then she turned to Francesca and, in a surprise move, hugged her, too.

And in even more of a surprise move Francesca hugged my mother back.

After our brief supportive-family moment my mother stepped away and said to both of us, "I'll call you tomorrow," then walked out the door without a backward glance.

Francesca and I watched the door for a long time. I don't know what she was looking for, but I half expected and half wished that my mother would come back. She didn't.

So before long, and without saying a word to each other, my sister and I went home.

Snafu

❧❀❧

Here's the thing about cataclysmic events: In between them life goes on, but not as usual. It's like a sci-fi story where it all *looks* right but there's something just a *bit* off about it, and you're not quite able to figure out what it is, and then when you do—*bam*—it's really scary.

One of the hardest parts of Life After the Stroke was trying to figure out how to act with the man who was my father and, at the same time, not my father.

Francesca had decided on the perky approach. She was always so cheerful with him; it drove me crazy. It was like she'd tapped into her inner six-year-old. Everything she said was punctuated with a minimum of two exclamation points.

"Hi, Daddy!!" she'd say. "How's it going!?! You look good!!!"

Which was *so* not true.

He looked anything but good. He looked old and bewildered, and he was easily startled, even by the familiar. Here's an example of what I mean:

He was sitting in his wheelchair in his hospital room one day. I walked in and said hello. He turned his head and looked at me, and I could see fear in his eyes for a moment. I realized with a jolt that he simply didn't know who I was. It took him a perceptible time chunk to work it out. It was like he'd turned his head faster than his brain could work.

Once he figured out who I was, though, he smiled his lopsided smile and reached out his left hand.

The first step closer was always the hardest. But once I had his hand in mine, I was okay.

I hadn't thought much about how Life After the Stroke must have been for my mother until the day, about a week or so after, when they moved my father out of intensive care and into the rehab center. That's when my mother started spending nights at home again and my sister went back to New Mexico.

"Call me if anything changes," she ordered my mother. "Don't keep anything from me."

My mother nodded wearily, and we stood in the drive-way and waved good-bye to Francesca.

As soon as her car disappeared down the hill, my mother and I broke into a "Good-bye Francesca" dance. We hopped and turned and shimmied. We clasped right hands and shook our left index fingers in the air. We chanted, "Don't keep anything from me!" as we waved our arms in the air in front of us.

For as long as I can remember, my mother and I have done dances to celebrate events both happy and sad. When I was really little, she'd pick me up to tango at random moments during the day. I learned to tango before I learned to walk. It's one of those things only she and I share.

Mokey ran in circles around us, barking and barking. When Jax pulled into the driveway, quite unexpectedly, he found us holding on to each other, laughing and gasping for breath.

"You girls okay?" asked Jax.

We nodded.

"You don't seem okay," said Jax.

We shook our heads.

"Don't keep anything from me," he said.

My mother and I looked at each other and exploded with laughter. We couldn't stop.

The next thing we knew, we were soaking wet and gasping, and Jax was standing beside us holding an empty bucket. The cold water sobered us up pretty fast, and we just stood there, dripping and staring at Jax in disbelief.

But only for a minute.

I grabbed the bucket from Jax so fast he had no time to protest, filled it quickly at the tap by the garage, then chased Jax around the driveway—but I couldn't catch him.

My mother signaled at me from behind his back. I saw that she was holding another full bucket. I slowed down. So did Jax. I walked forward, holding the bucket in front of me. Jax backed away. "Don't do it, Ange," he said, holding his hands out in front of him.

As if that would help!

I just kept skulking toward him, bringing him closer and closer to my mother. Then I put my bucket down.

"Okay," I said. "Okay. I won't throw my bucket of water at you."

"Good decision," he said.

"But I jolly well will!" said my mother. And then she did.

Now, Jax *dry* is cute—but Jax *wet* is awesome, with his hair plastered to his skull and his T-shirt clinging to his incredible logging bod.

Hmmmm. Guess I'd better buy him two buckets of condoms.

Later on we all sat in the living room eating popcorn while our clothes were in the dryer. My mother had popped *Bringing Up Baby* into the VCR, and we were watching Cary Grant jumping around in a negligee trimmed with marabou feathers.

"Me and Cary Grant," said Jax, stroking the terry tie around his waist, "wearing borrowed bathrobes." He'd changed into my father's bathrobe, and although my father wore it pretty well, Jax wore it better.

I wondered, as I thought about how good Jax would look if he could get into Cary's negligee, whether Jax was dreaming of getting into Cary's negligee in an entirely other way.

My mother was more relaxed than I had seen her in days, maybe years. And on her third glass of Merlot, my mother began to talk.

"Your father and I met at the wedding reception of a

mutual friend," she said, settling back into the cushions of the sofa and tucking her legs under her. A lock of her hair fell over her eyes, and she brushed it away. She had lit the table lamp, and I was struck by how young she looked in its soft light.

She said, "I had come with a date, who proceeded to get quietly snookered, then leave with one of the bridesmaids—the bloody wanker. I was sitting at the table alone, contemplating the wisdom of finishing the bits of wedding cake leftover on every plate on the table, when your father crossed the room and asked me to dance, thus saving me from gorging." She looked at me with a wry smile. Jax quietly reached for the remote and hit mute.

"What a distinguished, handsome man he was," my mother continued. "So virile. So imposing. He quite made me melt the very first time he put his hand on the small of my back and guided me onto the dance floor." She sighed, leaned back, and closed her eyes, remembering.

"Dancing with him was like no other dancing experience I'd had in my life—so effortlessly did he lead, so gracefully did he move. Gracefully, but never effeminately. Your father was masculine in all he did. Quite, quite the most masculine, virile man I've ever known." Her lips curled into a small, private smile.

She continued: "I went home with him that very night, and he proved his masculinity again in bed." She held her glass to her forehead and closed her eyes.

Whoa, Nelly. Weren't we getting a tad personal here?

I looked at Jax. He was fascinated and had actually picked up the wine bottle and filled my mom's glass again. He raised his eyebrows at me and smiled wickedly.

"We made love all night—"

Ahhhh!

"And in the morning I went home never expecting, really, to hear from him again. I'm so glad I was wrong about that." She giggled girlishly. I had never heard her giggle before, and I have never heard it since. In some ways it was more embarrassing than the sex talk.

"I hope, Angelina," said my mother, opening her eyes and focusing them, with some effort, on my face, "that someday you will find a man as attentive, as interested, as tender, as sensual as your father. That is my wish for you, Angelina." She turned and focused her eyes on Jax. "And it is my wish for you, too, Jax."

Jax's mouth dropped open.

"Of course I know," said my mother, smiling

affectionately at him. "Otherwise you would be dating my beautiful daughter."

Me? I looked at her in surprise.

"You *are* beautiful, you know," she said. "I haven't told you that enough. I know. That's just how I am. British reserve, I guess." She lifted her glass. "To you, my beautiful daughter!"

A drop of wine fell on her shirt. She licked her finger and rubbed uselessly at the stain, then shook her head in acceptance. Then she hiccupped, laid her head back on the chair, and closed her eyes. "Oh, Andrea," she said softly, more to herself, really, than to either of us. "Now what?"

As she sank deeper into the chair, Jax took the wine glass from her hand, and together we carried my mother upstairs and put her to bed.

Once we were back downstairs, Jax went to change back into his clothes, and we left the house. "Now, *that* was a side of your mother I've never seen before," he said as we walked toward his truck.

"And one I hope I never see again," I said.

"I don't know," said Jax. "I kinda liked it."

"I have an idea," I said brightly. "Next time let's get

your mother drunk and listen to her talk about her sex life with your dad, okay?"

Jax blushed.

"Hey," I said. "Do you think it's true?"

"What?" he asked.

"That you and I would be an item if you weren't gay?"

He looked at me.

"Maybe," he said.

I put my hands on his shoulders, stood on tiptoe, and kissed him on the lips. He kissed me back. No tongue or anything. Then we just held each other for a while.

When our moment was finished, he climbed into his truck and turned the key in the ignition. He let the engine idle for a minute and rolled down the window.

"Maybe," he said again, smiling, then he put the truck in gear and drove away.

Home Alone

After *my sister left,* my mother would drive to Burlington in the morning to see my father and then return home at night. I would come home after school, let the dog out, do my homework, watch a little TV. Then, when Mom came home, we'd eat. Often she'd bring takeout Chinese or pizza from a place in Burlington.

One night I decided to cook. I'd make hamburgers, fried potatoes, and a salad, the way my dad did when he cooked. I had never actually done it with him, but I'd watched him enough, I figured, to be able to handle it.

I sliced potatoes, put them in a pan with hot oil, shook oregano and garlic salt on them, covered them, and let them fry. Meanwhile, I rubbed the wooden bowl with raw garlic cloves. Six.

(My mother, in retelling this story, often ups the number of cloves for dramatic effect.)

I scooped some hamburger out of the bowl. The meat felt cold and fatty in my hands. As usual when handling raw meat, I reconsidered vegetarianism but put that decision off and put the burgers in the skillet instead.

I checked the potatoes and gave them another dose of garlic salt for good measure. Then I chopped up the salad and put it in the bowl, put mustard and oil in a cup measure, mixed it well, and poured it over the salad.

The hamburgers were sizzling when my mom walked in with the pizza.

"You're cooking?" she asked.

"Dad's burgers!" I said. "Dad's salad. Dad's potatoes."

She stopped dead and stared.

Then she nodded and put the pizza box on the counter, sat down, and said, "Serve 'em up."

I served.

We tasted.

As it turned out, the potatoes looked okay on the outside, but they were raw on the inside. The burgers had too much salt. And the salad? A vampire's worst nightmare.

After we spit our food out, my mother reached for the

pizza box. "Time to bring out the fallback meal," she said.

"I am *so* tired of this," I said, leaning my head on my hands and forcing back the pressure of a wave of tears. "I miss Dad."

My mother slid her chair back, came around the table, and stood beside me. She stroked my hair.

"Me too," she said. "Me too."

This little routine lasted for the three weeks Dad was in rehab, which was housed in another building right by the hospital. It was interrupted on the day before my father was to be moved to the Cold Hollow Rest Home, a convalescent facility in Winooski, close to the hospital. My mother wanted to spend the night in my father's room in order to ride to the home with him early the following morning.

"The question is," she said, "where are you going to stay?"

"Why can't I stay here?"

"All night, alone?" she asked.

"Why not?" I asked.

My mother looked me over for a long time, as if she were giving me an orbital character scan or something.

I held still, stood tall, and thought happy thoughts.

I must've passed the scan, because Mom said, "Okay."

"Can I invite Annika?" I asked.

"Can she stand to be away from James for that long?" asked Mom, raising an eyebrow.

"They have cell phones now, and that increases their geographical distance capabilities," I said.

Mom smiled and touched my cheek.

"Okay," she said.

I went up to my room to call Annika. Her cell voice mail picked up.

"Hi. This is Annika. I'm probably on the phone with James, so leave a message and I'll call you back."

"Call me back," I said, and hung up.

I was lying on my bed listening to the Beach Boys and waiting for Annika to call me back when my mom appeared in the doorway with her suitcase and said: "Did you reach Annika?"

"I left a message on her voice mail," I told my mother.

My mother just looked at me. I sat up.

"Don't worry, Mom," I said. "I'll be fine until she gets here."

My mother pressed her lips together, nodded, picked

up her bag, and turned to leave. Before taking even one step, she dropped her bag and, crossing the room to my bed, took my face in her hands and kissed me on the forehead. Then she turned and left, picking up her bag on the way out. I heard her footsteps going down the stairs, and I counted: There are eleven steps in our staircase, and before I got to eight, I was up off of my bed and standing at the top of the staircase.

"See you tomorrow, Mom," I said.

She turned when she got to the bottom and smiled at me.

"See you tomorrow," she said.

Not long after my mother left, I was in the kitchen rooting around for a snack when the phone rang. It was Annika.

"Sure," she said.

"Huh?" I said.

"I'd be up for staying with you tonight while your mom's away. Your mom called."

I looked at my watch. "No way," I said. "She's still in the car."

"On her cell," said Annika.

"What?" I said. Hey, when did she get a cell?

"Nah," said Annika. "Just kidding. She called from a gas station on her way and talked to my mom."

"Why did she call? I left a message for you," I said, feeling kind of miffed.

"Chill, Ange," said Annika. "She was taking care of you."

"I'm not a baby," I said, pouting.

"Well, you're sure acting like one," said Annika.

"Am not," I said.

"Are too," she said.

"Am not," I said.

"Are too," she said. "Oooops! Gotta go. My ride's here."

She disconnected, and I looked at the phone. "Am not," I said, and stuck out my tongue.

Anyway.

While I waited, I walked around the whole house. Mokey followed. We went into every room as I surveyed my kingdom.

Queendom.

Whatever.

I was standing by the door to the mudroom when Annika and James pulled up in James's old Toyota Corolla station wagon. He had to drive slowly to avoid hitting Mokey. I'd let him out earlier, and now he was running around the car and barking.

Finally James cut the engine, and he and Annika got out. As always, I felt a little like laughing when I saw them side by side. He's huge and she's tiny.

"Hey, Angelina," said James, and I waved back.

"So, James," Annika said, "pick me up tomorrow morning."

"I'll pick you up now," he said, and he did. He lifted her right up and they kissed. For a pretty long time.

I wouldn't be surprised if some tongue was involved.

After what seemed like an eternity I put my hands on my hips and began tapping my foot impatiently on the gravel. I stared at them until James put Annika down. Then he reached out a hand, squeezed my shoulder, and smiled.

"*Hasta la vista, señoritas,*" he said, and got back in his car and drove away.

"So, what are we going to do first?" Annika asked, following me into the kitchen and dropping her bag on the table.

"What do you see as our choices?" I asked.

"I know," said Annika. "Let's make a list. Got any paper?"

I opened our junk drawer and pulled out a pad and a stubby pencil and handed them to Annika.

"No," she said, pushing them away. "You write them. You have way better handwriting."

So I sat down at the table and wrote:

Home—Alone Activity Options

"Okay," she said. "One: We could drink ourselves sick."

I wrote:

1. Drink ourselves sick

"Two," she said. "We could invite boys over to spend the night."

I wrote:

2. Invite boys to spend the night

Then I looked at Annika and said, "Would you really spend the night with James here?"

Annika looked at me.

"I'd like to sleep with him," she said, "but not have sex with him."

"How come?" I asked. "You love him. He loves you.

Everyone knows the two of you are, like, meant for each other. You've been together since kindergarten."

"Yeah," she said. "That's part of it. We know we're going to be together for the rest of our lives, so we feel like we have to save something for later."

"How far do you go, then?" I asked.

"We touch each other with our hands," she said. "It's nice."

"I wish I had a boyfriend," I said.

"What about Jason?" Annika asked. "He's cute."

"He threw up on me in third grade," I reminded her. "I just don't want to kiss him."

"We have a serious boy shortage in our class," she said, shaking her head.

"Hey!" I said. "How come you didn't ask about Jax?"

Annika was quiet for a minute. Then she said softly: "Jax likes boys, doesn't he, Ange?"

"What makes you say that?" I asked.

"Because you're not his girlfriend, that's what," said Annika.

The conversation was on pause for a minute. Then I asked quietly, "Do you think everyone knows?"

"No one *knows*," said Annika, "but we all suspect."

"I do love him, you know," I said, "even a little like a boyfriend."

"Hmm," Annika said. "That's tough."

"Yeah. Well, anyway, maybe I'll meet someone in college," I said.

"Definitely. Now, back to the list," she said. "We could take the car and drive to Canada and drink and meet boys."

"No we couldn't," I said.

"Why not?" Annika asked. "I know how to drive."

"No car," I said.

"Right. Scratch that," she said.

She tapped her lips with her finger.

"I know," she said, reaching into her bag. "We could smoke a joint."

She pulled out a joint and a cigarette lighter and held them up.

"Let's go outside," I said.

We sat down on the doorstep, and Annika fired up the joint. We passed it back and forth between us for a while in silence. It was a clear night, not too cold. Across the driveway Midnight Rock shone silvery in the moonlight, like a hole in the world: a space, a void.

Tears pricked my eyes as I handed Annika the doobie and stood up.

"I want to show you something," I said, and I took her hand and pulled her after me to the rock.

"This is Midnight Rock," I said. We regarded it in silence. Then I said, "What do you think?"

"It's a rock," she said.

"It's not *just* a rock," I said.

"Heck, no!" said Annika. "It's a frickin' huge rock."

"This rock has a history," I said.

"Like every other rock doesn't?" asked Annika, smirking. "And your point is . . ."

"My father and I have been coming out here at night to look at the stars my whole life," I said. "This is where he taught me how to recognize Orion and the Pleiades. We used to lie out here and watch the Perseids burn across the cosmos."

"Burn across the cosmos?" said Annika.

"Shut up," I said. "I'm waxing eloquent."

"Wax away," she said.

This struck us as hilarious, and we started laughing.

"Would you like to sit on Midnight Rock with me?" I asked.

"Sure," said Annika.

We sat.

"No one has ever sat on Midnight Rock with me before," I said. "I mean, aside from my father."

"Not even your mom?" asked Annika.

"Especially not my mom," I said. "This is my special spot with my father." I sighed. "I wonder if I'll ever get to lie out here with him again."

Annika put her arm around me. "He'll be okay," she said.

"Yeah," I said.

But I didn't exactly believe it.

The two of us lay down side by side on Midnight Rock and looked up at the sky. The moon hung just above the trees, and it was so full and so bright that it almost hurt to look at it. The stars nearby looked washed out and old in comparison.

It felt a little weird to be lying next to someone other than my father—but it also felt good having Annika there. "The sky is not ours, Dad," I thought, only I must have said it out loud, because Annika turned to me and said, "Huh?"

"Nothing," I said. "Just . . . something."

And it was either because we were both buzzed or because she just wasn't listening all that closely that this seemed to make perfect sense to us both.

Much later that night—or really early the next morning, since it was about 1 a.m.—Annika and I were watching *Alien* and munching popcorn. The alien had just punched a hole in John Hurt's gut when Mokey lifted his head and cocked an ear.

"What is it, boy?" I asked.

Annika turned down the volume, and we both shifted into active listening mode.

And then we heard it: the crunching of footsteps on the gravel in the driveway. Mokey ran to the back door and barked and barked and barked.

"Who could be walking up here at this time of night?" whispered Annika.

The footsteps continued. We dropped down and crawled to the window and peeked out.

A man was walking down the driveway. He was still pretty far away, but he was big. And alone.

Annika and I sat down with our backs against the wall under the windowsill.

"I'm going to call 911," I said as I started crawling toward the kitchen.

"Wait!" she said. "We can use my cell. It's right here." She pulled her cell phone out of the pocket of her jeans and flipped it open. "A text message from James," she said.

"What's it say?" I asked.

"'I'm on my way,'" she read. "Hmm!"

She got up on her knees and peered out the window again.

"That's him," she said, and she stood up and opened the front door. "What are you doing?" she yelled. "Where's your car?"

"I just wanted to check on you and be sure you were safe, but I didn't want to wake you if you were asleep," he said. "So I left the car down the road a ways and walked."

"You didn't want to wake us, but you weren't at all worried about scaring us half to death?" she asked.

"Sorry," he said. "Didn't think about that."

Annika went out and gave James a kiss on the cheek.

"Thanks for worrying about us enough to check on us," she said. "Now, go home."

James waved to me, turned, and walked back up the driveway.

"You sure you really want a boyfriend?" Annika asked as we went back inside and closed—and locked—the door behind us.

The Top Three Epiphanies

H*ere is a list of* the top three epiphanies in my life so far:

1. The discomfort of my first glimpse of what "infinity" means: age seven. I remember I was lying on the grass in front of our house looking up at the sky and thinking, *The sky never ends,* then imagining someone installing a brick ceiling for the sky, then asking myself (through I already knew the answer): *What's on top of the ceiling?* Then thinking maybe dinosaurs (a whole Paleolithic ecosystem, in fact) but having to ultimately grudgingly admit that no matter how many brick ceilings were constructed and no matter what was on top of each, there would always be more sky above. I hated this idea, but at the same time I was—and am—awed by it.

2. Suddenly realizing that Ho Jo stands for Howard

Johnson: age fifteen. I'm not proud of this, but it happens to be a shining, if embarrassing, revelation in my life.

3. Age is relative: age sixteen. Relative to the Blodgett parent population, my father was an antique. Ancient. He may as well have been Methuselah himself, he was so old.

Relative to the population at the Cold Hollow Rest Home, where he went after he left the hospital, my father was a mere whippersnapper, a shirttail lad, an infant. His roommate, Mr. Simmons, for example, out-olded him by roughly thirty years. I began to feel almost normal there, generationally speaking.

"There's the lovely young lady," said Mr. Simmons every time I entered my father's room for a visit. Mr. Simmons was tiny and frail. He had a lot of white, white hair, a trim white beard, and perfect teeth. They were, of course, false. He dressed every day in polyester slacks with one of those barely perceptible woven patterns, a slightly yellowed white button-down shirt, and an ascot. His blue eyes were a bit filmy but still lively. There was always white stuff gathered in the corners of his eyes and his lips, which he wiped away with a bright white handkerchief when he thought of it. He was very tidy, very put-together for someone his age—as if he felt a need to be presentable for someone, even though he never seemed to have any visitors. Whenever I took my father out of the room, I always felt sorry for Mr. Simmons, alone and fragile and old and left behind.

A nursing home is not the most depressing place on Earth, but it's got to be close. The halls always smell of vegetable soup and medication and sometimes other things. It's like the smell of waiting. People in nursing homes are all just waiting: waiting for meds, waiting for people who come, waiting for people who never come, waiting to recover, and waiting to die. When I visited my father, I was always keenly aware that it was the next-to-last category we were hoping for, but the last category we were afraid would be the truth.

I brought Jax with me on one of my visits.

"There's the lovely young lady," said Mr. Simmons when we walked into the room. He was seated on the edge of my father's bed. My father was dressed and propped up against his pillows, his wheelchair rolled close enough to get him into it with a minimum amount of trouble. "I was just reminiscing with your father about the golden days of Hollywood, back when stars were Stars . . . but I think he's too young to remember." Mr. Simmons chuckled. My father rolled his eyes.

Apparently, about a hundred years ago Mr. Simmons used to write for the movies. He once told me the titles of some of the movies he'd written. I didn't recognize the name of a single one.

Jax cleared his throat to remind me that he was there, and I said: "This is my friend Jax. And Jax, this is Mr. Simmons."

Mr. Simmons stood up and extended his hand. There was an old-world elegance in his movements. Jax shook hands with him.

"I understand you used to write for the movies, sir," said Jax, who can be as polite as Eddie Haskell when the situation calls for it.

"I wrote additional dialogue for *The Divorcée* with Norma Shearer," said Mr. Simmons. "Ever hear of it?" He said this as if it was a challenge. A dare.

Jax said, "Yes."

"I wouldn't be surprised if you hadn't heard of it," said Mr. Simmons, completely ignoring Jax's answer.

Jax and I exchanged a shrug and a smile.

My father pointed to his wheelchair with his chin and said, "Ho, ho!"

I helped him guide himself into the seat, then pushed him toward the door.

"Coming, Jax?" I asked.

"I think I'll stay here and visit with Mr. Simmons," said Jax. "I really want to hear about Jackie Coogan. That's the original Uncle Fester, you know!"

"*Hasta la vista*, then," I said, and wheeled my father out of the room. I didn't have to feel sorry for Mr. Simmons today; it was Blissville for him and Jax both, pure and simple.

My father pointed the way with his good hand and led us into the common room, which was, as always, empty. Ever the congenial host, my father gestured for me to sit in one of the orange armchairs. I wheeled him next to one by the window and took a seat.

(Why is orange the color of choice for institutional furniture?)

"Ho ho!" said my father, indicating the view beyond the French doors as if he were personally responsible for it.

It was Vermont at its best: a rolling lawn; some trees in orange and red hues; black-and-white Holsteins in an impossibly green pasture; a meandering brook; a big, old sugarhouse; and beyond that, Lake Champlain and the Adirondacks.

"If any place could make you recover by sheer force of scenery, this place could," I said to my father.

He laughed and pulled me down for a kiss. I felt myself clutch up and fought the urge to resist. He smelled old, and that made me sad.

"Where's Mom?" I asked, quickly regretting it.

"Ho, ho," said my father, pointing out into the hall somewhere.

"Outside?" I asked.

He shook his head.

"Ho! Ho ho!" he said, pointing again.

"Car?" I tried.

My father shook his head again.

"Ho. Ho ho ho!" he insisted, losing his patience, waving his hand up toward the ceiling.

"Looking for a nurse?" I guessed.

My father shouted, "*Ho Ho Ho!*" and angrily grabbed my arm and shook me. Hard. He was strong. That surprised me. His face was red, and he was gritting his teeth, he was so angry. I was a little scared of him then, and I slid to the far side of the chair. I wasn't sure, but I felt like he was saying, "Get with the program! Use your brain!"

I shook my head and started to feel tears at the top of

my nose. "I don't know, Daddy," I said. "I'm sorry. I don't understand."

"He means the bathroom," said my mother.

We turned to look at her, standing in the doorway.

My father sighed and looked defeated.

I felt beaten, and I hung my head. My mother took my father's hand and looked everywhere but at me.

We sat in silence for a while.

"That Mike Simmons is a walking resource on the golden age of Hollywood," Jax said on the way home. "He knew Gloria Swanson." He shook his head in admiration. "Gloria Swanson! Think of it. I'm taking a video camera next time and getting this stuff on tape."

I still didn't say anything.

"You okay?" he asked.

I shook my head.

"My father tried to tell me something today, and I didn't understand it," I said. "Not at all."

Jax put his arm around me and pulled me closer to him on the car seat. I laid my head on his shoulder.

"And that's not the worst part," I said. "The worst part is that at first I didn't know what to feel . . . frustration or sadness. And then I felt . . . pity!" The word fell out of my mouth like a toad. Barely audible. But true.

I pitied my father. And I knew he'd never want to be pitied by anyone.

For the first time I felt like I truly understood why he might want to pull out his tubes.

Mothers vs. Fathers

As a small child, I guess I must have loved my mom as much as my dad did. His love for her was so big that you couldn't help being swept up by it. But as I got older and the conflict between me and my mom amped up, I started to feel less loving. This is probably normal between moms and daughters, but in a house like ours, where the parental units had such an ironclad bond, any deviation from the feeling of love showed up in stark relief.

I remember one night we were out at Midnight Rock, my father and I. I had just had a particularly bad run-in with my mom. Not that long ago, actually. She'd objected to the way I spoke. I remember I was telling her a story:

"And Jax was like, 'Let's go to the football game,' and I was like, 'Well, when is it?' And he goes, 'Saturday at two,' and I was all, 'I can't. I have to go to Burlington—"

"Stop!" cried my mother. "What is this 'like' and 'goes' and 'all' business? He *said*. You *said*. Not 'like.' Not 'goes.' Not 'all.' It makes you sound stupid."

"That is so insulting!" I said, running outside.

As I slammed the door and walked a few steps from the house, I could hear my father murmuring to my mother, but I couldn't make out what he was saying.

In search of comfort, I decided to lie down on Midnight Rock, which was still warm from the sun. I leaned back on my arms, looked at the stars, and thought about my mother.

What did she want from me, anyway? I was just a twenty-first-century American kid! I was so angry I started to cry. Soon I heard the door open and close, and then I felt my father lower himself down beside me.

"We have not been out here in many years, *cara mia*," he said to me.

I didn't say anything.

"There are some of our old friends, I see," he said. "Cassiopeia. The Seven Sisters. Orion. And look. There on the horizon is Draco."

I still didn't say anything.

My father took my hand.

"You must not be too critical of your mother," he said softly. "Your mother wants you to be elegant, polished, lovely—a lady."

"She's not nice," I said. "She's not nice to me."

My father did not respond immediately. Then he said, "Perhaps that is so, *cara mia*," which surprised me. I mean, I guess I thought he'd argue with me on that point. I turned to look at him. He took my chin in his hand and looked into my eyes. "But she is loyal," he said, "and someday you will understand that loyalty is more valuable than niceness."

"I am who I am, Daddy," I said defiantly. "Why can't she love me the way I am?"

"She does, *cara mia*," he said. "She just has a hard time showing it."

"She doesn't have a hard time showing it to you," I said, and I was immediately sorry and embarrassed that I'd said that. It was totally different. I knew.

My father contemplated me for a while, then a smile curled the corners of his lips. He smoothed my hair.

"You are a smart girl, my Angelina," he said. "Your mother is a good woman, despite her ways. She loves you. She will always do her duty by you. You must learn to accept *her* for who *she* is."

"She should learn that about me, too," I said peevishly as tears started rolling down my cheeks. I couldn't help it.

"Perhaps she will," said my father. "Perhaps she will."

He took a breath and looked at me.

"But I wouldn't hold my breath," he added with a mischievous little smile that made his eyes crinkle and twinkle. He brushed my tears away with his thumbs.

"Don't cry for this, Angelina," he sang softly.

We both laughed.

Do you have any question about why I love my father so much?

When I remember this night, I imagine my mother looking out the kitchen window, a rectangle of warm, golden light in the dark night, seeing us and perhaps feeling jealous.

But I only imagine this. I don't know if it actually happened.

Pity A

My father did not die in Cold Hollow Rest Home. He didn't get much better, but he didn't get much worse, so after a month of therapies that I'm not sure made any difference at all—I mean, he still couldn't walk or talk—he was allowed to come home.

I'm sorry to say that I greeted the news of his homecoming with less joy than you'd expect. The fact was, I didn't totally want him to come home. I mean, I definitely wanted life back to normal—but I didn't think that was going to happen anytime soon. And I'd gotten used to being alone in the house between the time I got home from school and the time my mother got in from her duties at my father's side.

Anyway.

Here's how I got the news.

One afternoon I jumped off the bus and ran down the embankment to our driveway. It was a mild, overcast day with the smell of snow in the air. I remember thinking that I would take Mokey for a long walk up the road. I remember wondering whether or not to invite Jax and then have to wait for him to come, or just grab the dog and go while the spirit moved me. I decided on option two and opened the door.

The first thing I noticed was that Mokey's kennel was empty. Then I heard my mother's voice from the kitchen.

"Angelina!" she called.

"Mom!" I said. "What are you doing here?"

Of course, this is not what I meant exactly. I mean, after all, it is her house, and I certainly didn't mean to sound that unwelcoming. But it's what I said. And actually, I felt that unwelcoming.

I walked sullenly into the kitchen. My mother was waiting for me at the table. She sighed. Deeply.

"Sit down, Angelina," she said. She looked beat. Mokey was sitting on her lap, and she was scratching his chin absently. I pulled out my chair and sat down opposite her.

"Your father is coming home," she said.

"When?" I asked.

She sighed heavily again. She looked around the kitchen distractedly, then fixed her eyes on me.

"As soon as we can get the house ready," she said. "About another month."

"Ramps?" I asked.

She nodded.

Ramps, of course, were just the tip of the iceberg.

From that day on, the carpenters were at work 24/7 in our house—or so it seemed. We must've been paying big bucks to have them come so quickly and work so steadily. I awoke to hammering and sawing and fell asleep with sawdust in my nose.

They changed the room off the garage, once my father's old woodworking room, into a bedroom. A guy who has the use of only one arm doesn't need a jigsaw or a router or an electric sander. He needs a shower stall with a bench, he needs a toilet with a support railing, he needs handicapped access to the outdoors.

Anyway, they gutted the space, then rebuilt it to accommodate the new Andrea. The house had to change to remain his home. And me? Well, it took me a while not to feel gutted myself; how much could my life change and still remain my life?

In English, the day before the construction started, we had to write haiku poems. Here's mine:

She sold all his tools
And put in a ramp or two,
And then he came home.

I got an A. But I think it was a pity A.

Paradox on Earth

And then . . . well, he came home.

The end.

Of my life as I knew it, that is.

And it was the beginning of a life that was paradox intensive. The main paradox, of course, was that whole end-equals-beginning thing, but there were other things too, like

- easier and harder,
- happier and unhappier,
- more stressful and less stressful,
- there and not there.

I'll take them in order.

Easier and harder:

Of course, the long daily commute to Burlington was over, and that was definitely easier for my mom—and for me too, I guess. I mean, I didn't have to take care of the dog after school anymore or attempt to cook again. Not that I really did after the burger incident.

Then again, someone was there when I got home from school: my father. This definitely bled over into the harder side.

Which brings us to the next paradox.

Happier and unhappier:

My father was home, and I was happy he wasn't in the hospital anymore, but my father's presence in the house was a real downer. It was heavy. It was oppressive.

My father wasn't always home when I was a kid. As I said, he worked for this major Italian import/export company, and the headquarters were located in New York City. He flew out every Monday morning and flew home every Friday afternoon. He basically only spent weekends with us until I was about ten, and then he retired.

I remember how I looked forward to Fridays because I knew that when I got home, he'd be waiting. He might be sitting in the living room reading the local paper, or out on the back porch assembling the hammock after a winter of storage, or maybe starting to prepare dinner for us.

Fast-forward to Life After the Stroke, and I was likely to find him in his wheelchair sitting in the kitchen watching my mother prepare dinner, or in his wheelchair in front of the TV, or in his wheelchair sleeping by the French doors and drooling in a shaft of weak winter sunlight.

Once I found him in his wheelchair sitting in the doorway to the mudroom while my mom shoveled snow off the porch. He looked translucent in the sunlight. His fine white hair stuck out from under his hat, his body looked small in his jacket, his legs almost invisible under a blanket, and his feet looked fake in a pair of bright white running shoes with Velcro straps.

There's something pathetic about shoes on the feet of people who don't walk.

Anyway, when she saw me, my mother pushed a lock of her brown hair off her face and smiled.

"I thought your father could use some fresh air," she said. "Would you like to help?"

Was my mother actually inviting me to join their two-some? These days more than ever, they spent nearly every waking minute together, locked into each other on a whole different level.

I looked at my father. He winked at me.

I looked at my mother, extending the snow shovel in my direction.

I dropped my backpack and took it.

After we finished, after my mother had swept the last crystals of snow off the porch, I ran inside to get my camera, and I took a picture of my mom and dad, Mom holding the broom, Dad framed in the doorway. My mother's eyelashes were frosty, and she had a bad case of hat hair, but she looked healthy and alive. My father looked old and wispy, but he regarded the camera with a twinkle in his eye.

Back to the list.

More stressful and less stressful:

It was less stressful, especially for my mom, because she didn't have to go to Burlington anymore. No more driving. No more hours in the nursing home. No more worrying that my father would die while she was not there.

More stressful for all of us because when he came home, we knew he might die at home. Plus, he needed so much help.

There and not there:

It wasn't really my father, you know? I mean, it sort of looked like him, and it wore his clothing, but it *wasn't* him.

Anyway.

The day he came home, my mother told me I had to be there to greet him, so after school Jax drove me home. My mom and dad hadn't gotten back yet, so Jax and I hung out in my dad's fabulous new room. We threw ourselves down on his bed and flicked on the television with the remote. I surfed the channels.

Jax rolled over on his back and laced his fingers behind his head.

"You think your mom will be wandering down the stairs at night to sleep with your father down here?" he asked.

"I don't know," I said. "What do you think?"

"I don't know," he said. "I mean, what could they do? Your dad's paralyzed."

"Jax, please!" I said. I was still recovering from my recent trip down Mom's sexual memory lane.

"Don't tell me you haven't thought about it," he said, smiling mischievously.

I didn't say anything, but I had thought about it.

"Jax," I said.

"Still here," he said.

"Have you ever really thought about us?" My heart was pounding, and I couldn't even figure out why I had asked such a thing. I wanted to take it back. But I didn't.

For a long time Jax didn't say anything; he just stared at the ceiling while I stared at him, trying to read his mind, I guess. Maybe. Maybe not. Maybe it was just because he is so easy to stare at.

He sighed. And then all he said, kind of sadly, was "Angelina."

"Forget it," I said. "It was a stupid question. I'm sorry. "

"It's not that," he said. "It's just that, well, I *have* thought about us . . . like that."

I just stared at him.

"When I was younger," he told me, not looking at me, "when I was still trying to convince myself that I was straight, well, I used to make myself, you know, imagine having sex with a girl, and the only girl I ever imagined was you."

"Really?" I asked.

He nodded.

I didn't know what to feel about this. I mean, sure, I'd always wanted to hear Jax tell me he had those kinds of thoughts about me, but not exactly like this.

"You had to 'make' yourself fantasize about me?" I asked.

"Well, I don't mean it in a bad way," he said, "but, you know, you were no Jason."

And that's when I hit him in the face with a pillow.

Then he hit me, and suddenly we were in the middle of a pillow fight. We were laughing so hard we almost didn't hear the door open and my mother calling me.

"Angelina!" came my mother's voice. "Where are you? Come and say hello to your father."

I quickly shut the TV off and walked slowly out into the mudroom, Jax right behind me.

My father was sitting in his wheelchair. He looked so diminished, so small. But he also looked happy. Happy to be home, I figured. And in retrospect I realize that he, too, must have been caught up in at least one of the same paradoxes I was—happy to be home, but also unhappy to be, if you know what I mean.

He extended his left hand to me, and I took it. He squeezed my hand, then let it go and reached for Jax, who took his hand and leaned down and gave my father a kiss on both cheeks, Euro style.

"Come see your new room, Andrea," said my mother, pushing his chair across the mudroom and down the ramp.

My father looked around. He took in the new bed, the big TV, the seat in the shower, the rail by the toilet. He shut his eyes and hid behind his eyelids for a minute. When he opened them, he looked resigned. He gave a sad sort of smile and nodded.

"Ho ho," he said, gesturing with his left arm.

"You're welcome," said my mother.

The rest of that afternoon passed in slo-mo. There was a thickness about time; as if we were all moving through clear gelatin. My mother was hyperaware of my father and where he was at all times. She left him alone only for short periods, and even then she continually peeked around doorways to make sure he was okay. I tiptoed as if there were a very light sleeper in the house whom I was afraid of waking, and in a figurative way, I guess, there was. It was me. I wasn't ready to embrace all this.

To distract myself, I mostly stayed in my room and did my homework or listened to music. Once, a day or so after my father had come home, I actually succeeded in forgetting he was there altogether. I was lying on my bed reading about Vermont during the Industrial Revolution, and I guess I must've fallen asleep—social studies has this effect on me.

Anyway.

I woke up at 7 p.m. when I heard my mother calling me for dinner. When I walked into the kitchen, I just stopped dead in the doorway: My father was sitting in a wheelchair by the table. So unusual, but also so ordinary. It took me a minute to realign the reality perimeter.

Dinner was often stressful with my father. No surprise there; I think we'd all expected it.

First of all, the food was only so-so. One night my mother prepared some pasta using a canned sauce. We also had frozen garlic bread, and she used store-bought dressing on the salad. My father dropped a lot of sauce on the front of his shirt and plenty of lettuce into his lap. My mother tried to help him eat, but he got mad and waved her away. I spent most of the dinner looking at my food.

After dinner we sat awkwardly around the living room. My mother turned on the radio, and we listened to an NPR drone talk about the latest lawsuit against cigarette companies by longtime smokers and cancer victims. My father suddenly raised his head and really paid attention.

When the report was over, he started shouting, "Ho ho ho ho ho ho!" and gesturing like a maniac. He got our attention.

My father clenched his fist and tried again, pointing to the radio and shaking his head.

"Ho ho ho ho ho!" he said louder.

"You take issue with the report?" asked my mother.

My father nodded and shouted some more, then grabbed a small ceramic figurine of a shepherdess off the lamp table and hurled it across the room. It shattered against the wall, and Mokey barked at it.

My mother and I glanced at each other, then back at my father. His head was hanging and he looked ashamed. I didn't know what had just happened; I don't think my mom knew either.

My father took a deep breath, then looked up. He gestured toward the bedroom.

My mother nodded. I sat quietly, hoping not to be noticed.

No such luck.

"Say good night to your father," said my mother.

"Good night, Daddy," I said.

"Ho ho," he said, touching his cheek.

He wanted me to kiss him. . . .

The split second it took me to realize that I should go ahead and kiss my father did not go unnoticed, and I saw the hurt in his eyes. I crossed the room and pecked him on the cheek. As I pulled my face away, he caught my chin in his left hand and held my face just a few inches from his own. He looked deeply into my eyes, and I was forced to look deeply into his. And do you know what I saw? I saw my father in there.

It was a totally loaded moment.

He touched my cheek with the back of his hand, then slowly wheeled out of the room, my mother following.

Helping Daddy Pee

*O*nce upon a time there was a girl whose father had a stroke. He had to go to the bathroom, and the girl's mother, who usually took him, was in the shower. So the little girl wished for her fairy godmother to show up and do it for her, and she did, and so the little girl was able to finish her breakfast.

Well—not quite.

It was early in the morning. My mother was in the shower. My father had just finished his breakfast and was parked by the French doors, looking out over our back fields to the mountains beyond. I rinsed my own cereal bowl and was bending to pick up my backpack when my father ho-hoed. I looked up. He jerked his left thumb toward his room, then nodded.

"You want to go to your room?" I asked.

He nodded again.

I took his wheelchair and turned him around, and he rolled off slowly, navigating down one ramp and up another into his room.

"Want the TV on?" I asked.

He shook his head emphatically, then pointed to the bathroom.

And then came the dawn, as they say.

He needed to use the bathroom.

"Want to brush your teeth?" I asked in a last-ditch effort to control reality: Was I really going to help my dad pee?

He shook his head again and looked at me, and I think, looking back, that he was more embarrassed than I was—though if you'd told me that at that moment, I wouldn't have believed you. As I mentioned earlier, in our house we have never been very modest. My father is Italian, for cripe's sake. They go nude to the beach, and the women never shave. When I was little, we all showered together—even Mom. But the idea of taking him to the bathroom to pee was not quite the same.

I nodded and pressed my lips together.

Wait, I thought. *What about Mom?*

"Just a minute," I said.

I stuck my head out his bedroom door and listened hard. The shower was still going. Shoot. I could not call in the First Battalion.

I turned back to face him.

"Ummmm," I said, "Mom's still in the shower. Can't you wait for her to finish? She never takes long showers. You know that."

He looked at me reprovingly.

"Ho ho hoho *ho*, ho hoho *ho*," he said, raising his eyebrows and giving me a mischievous grin.

"When you gotta go, you gotta go," I said, and I had to smile.

We laughed together, and it felt good. Broke the ice.

I followed his wheelchair bathroomward.

Now what? I thought as we wheeled into the bathroom.

I pushed him toward the bowl. He reached down and unzipped his fly. At first I thought he was going to try to aim while he was sitting, but then he reached out his left hand for me. I hesitated. He reached again. I stepped forward. He held on to my shoulder, put his left foot on the floor, and pushed himself to a standing position, leaning heavily on me. Through some superhuman effort I managed to stay upright.

Now it gets really weird.

So he was using his left hand to steady himself on me, so he couldn't, you know, take out his penis and hold it, which meant . . . well, I didn't even want to think about what it meant.

Fortunately, my father had another plan.

"Ho ho," he said, jerking his head to the right.

Huh?

He took his left hand and pushed me behind him.

He wanted me to stand behind him and steady him at the waist.

Carefully, slowly, he removed his hand from my shoulder. Carefully, slowly, I inched my way behind him and put my arms around his waist and braced myself to hold him. I leaned my cheek against his back and stared at the floor.

I felt him move his left hand, I heard his pee hit the water, I felt him zip.

"Ho ho," he said.

I inched my way carefully and slowly around so I was in front of him again, and eased him back into his chair.

I flushed, then wheeled him over to the sink, turned on the tap, pumped some soap onto his palm, and washed his hand. He rinsed and dried, then reached out, took my chin in his hand, and forced me to look him in the eye. Then he smiled at me.

I didn't smile back. I was still feeling too bizarre.

"Dad," I said. "How weird was that for you?"

He shrugged and pulled my face to his and kissed the tip of my nose like he did when I was a baby.

My mother walked into Dad's bedroom.

"Andrea?" she called.

She peeked into the bathroom and immediately understood what had happened.

"How did it go?" she asked.

"Ho ho hoho *ho*, ho hoho *ho*," my father said.

"Pardon?" said Mom.

"When you gotta go, you gotta go," I said, and my father and I gave each other the thumbs-up.

My mother looked at the two of us, sizing us up, I guess, then she smiled wryly and shook her head.

"Well," she said, "I'm no historian, but this has to be one of the more unusual father/daughter moments in the history of father/daughter moments." She paused and smiled again, then said, "Thank you, Angelina."

Maybe I wouldn't be voted off the island after all.

Meanwhile, Back at School...

S o, *Celeste hated me.* And I didn't know why. We've established that.

Obviously, I hated Celeste because she hated me.

It's not much of a reason, I know, but it's the only one I had.

So you can imagine my surprise when she stopped me in the hall between classes a few days after my father came home.

"Rossini," she said.

I immediately stepped into my metaphorical defensiveness shoes. I think of them as a cross between combat boots and black platform flip-flops.

"What?" I said.

"You know those free coffee coupons we got?" she asked.

"Yeah . . . ," I said. Did she want mine?

"Well, I was thinking you and I could, like, redeem them," she said. "Together."

Whoa.

Had Celeste just used the word "redeem" in a sentence? And more important: Was Celeste asking me to go out for coffee with her?

"Huh?" I said. "Are you asking me to go out for coffee with you?"

Celeste stepped away from me. "Look," she said, and her voice had an edge, "if you don't want to, just say so!"

Did I want to?

I must have, because I heard myself say: "Sure." And then, "When?"

"This afternoon?" she said. "After school?"

"Okay," I said. "Yeah."

Then we stood around awkwardly for a few seconds, not sure how to end this friendly encounter. I mean, our usual form of farewell involved fisticuffs, which seemed inappropriate here.

Finally I said: "See you later, then."

And she said: "Yeah." But she still stood there.

And I said: "Well, bye. I have to go to English now."

And she said: "Yeah, bye."

And I walked away, but when I looked back, Celeste was still standing there.

What in the world could Celeste possibly have to say to me that she wouldn't prefer to shout in front of the entire Blodgett High School student body? In a way, I was looking forward to finding out.

Jax met me just outside the English classroom.

"Need a ride home after school?" he asked.

"No, thanks," I said. "I'm meeting Celeste for coffee at Sugar's."

I waited to see what effect this factoid would have on Jax.

Basically it had no effect.

"Did you hear what I said?" I asked.

"Yeah," he said.

"Aren't you even surprised at all?" I asked.

"Hell, yeah," he said. "I'm just too manly to show it."

I slugged him in the arm, and we went into class.

After school I started off down the path to town. The path goes from the school driveway, through a patch of woods, across the rec field, then it connects with Main Street. Before I got very far, Annika and James caught up with me. They always walk home that way; they both live downtown.

"We hear you're going to have coffee with Celeste," Annika said. "What's the story?"

"I don't know," I said.

"Look!" said James, jerking his chin toward a spot down the hill. "There she is."

And there she was, crossing the soccer field. She was alone. We stopped and waited until she turned the corner onto Main Street.

"So, what do you think she wants to talk to me about?" I asked when we began walking again.

Annika and James were slightly ahead of me, dappled by the afternoon sunlight dropping through the bare branches. Annika let go of James's hand. He stopped and looked at her questioningly. She gave him a little push, and he kept on walking. She and I fell into step together.

"You have any ideas?" she asked me.

"Jax," I said.

"You think she has a crush on him?" asked Annika.

I shrugged.

"Nahhh." James threw this comment back over his shoulder at us.

"Huh?" we said.

"Celeste isn't interested in boys," said James.

"No way!" I said.

"Way!" James replied.

"You mean we have a gay guy *and* a lesbian in our school?" Annika almost shrieked. "For a small town, we are so diverse!"

"It makes sense," I said. "I mean, she's been hanging around with Walker since first grade, but he's not her boyfriend."

"Walker likes Roxie," said James.

"Yeah, and she'll never go anywhere with him," said Annika.

"Why would she, when she has a boy like Jason as her sex slave?" James said.

"What's it like to have a sex slave?" I wondered, picking my way sideways down a steep part of the trail, using exposed roots as steps.

"It's awesome!" said James. Annika punched him in the arm. He caught her fist, then lifted her up, kissed her, and set her down. We walked for a while in silence.

Then Annika said, "Maybe she has a crush on you."

Oh.

*   *   *

Celeste was waiting for me at the counter. I saw her chatting with Erin, the Dorcas of the afternoon shift. Erin graduated from BHS a couple of years ago. She works here some afternoons and at the video place others. In the winter she also teaches snowboarding. Her boyfriend, Brad, makes snow at Jay Peak. They are your typical young northern-Vermont couple.

The two of them were laughing together when I walked up.

"Hey!" said Erin.

Celeste said, "Hi."

"We were just talking about that time at summer camp when Celeste and you and Annika built a hotel for fairies, while the rest of us were making shelters for, you know, squirrels," said Erin.

I smiled. I hadn't thought about that in years.

"And you," she said, looking at me, "built them an outhouse."

It was true.

"We were weirdos in first grade," I said.

"Yeah," said Celeste, and she smiled and blushed.

We ordered coffee and doughnuts and gave Erin our coupons. Then we sat down.

"I forgot all about the fairy outhouse," I said.

"I didn't," said Celeste.

Erin set our order down in front of us and went back to the kitchen.

I added cream and sugar to my coffee.

Celeste sipped hers black.

I tasted my coffee, then added more sugar.

Finally I said: "Did you want to talk to me about something special?"

Celeste fiddled with her cup.

"I wanted to ask your advice," she said.

What in the world could Celeste possibly need my advice on?

"On how to handle a crush on someone you know will never return it," she continued.

"I guess I'm something of an expert on that," I said. I sipped my coffee. Too sweet.

"So how do you handle it?" she asked.

"Sometimes better than others, I have to say," I said.

"Do you ever get angry?" she said. "Sometimes I feel so angry I just want to punch something," she said. She clenched her fist, and I thought she was going to bang it on the table, but she didn't.

"Not anymore," I said. "I used to, though. Then I went through this whole harangue phase where I thought that if I just argued with him enough, he'd change. I don't have to tell you how successful that campaign was."

Celeste smiled. She picked up her doughnut and began crumbling it between her fingers and letting the crumbs fall into her coffee.

"Did you ever tell him your feelings?" she asked.

"Sure," I said. "Lots of times."

"Did it help?" she asked.

"No," I said. "Not really."

"So it's not something you'd recommend, then?" she asked.

"Well," I said, "if you want to be friends and keep the air clear, I think you have to talk about it."

Celeste nodded. She lifted her cup to her lips and sipped, then chewed, her coffee for a minute. I tried it with my doughnut. It wasn't bad. Then I said, "So, are you and this person friends?"

"No," she said.

"Could you be?" I asked.

"I don't know," she said. "Could we?" She looked straight into my eyes, then looked away.

Oh, my God!

Annika was right.

Celeste had a crush on me.

No one had ever had a crush on me before. My first thought was *This is great!*

My second thought: *Whoa! This is* so *not great.*

"I'm not a lesbian," I said, and Celeste shot me a look of the purest contempt and stood up.

"I guess we can't," she said, and made her way through the tables and out the door.

True Communication

My father was on the Blodgett School Board, but after his stroke my mother took over his seat. My father had been home almost a month, actually, when my mother decided she would attend the next meeting.

"Who's staying with Dad?" I asked.

"You are," said my mother.

"Do I have to?" I asked.

"Are you whining?" asked my mother.

"Yes," I said. "I believe that this is a situation that calls for some serious whining."

My mother looked at me and said, "You know, Angelina. I believe you're right. Let's whine together."

I looked at my mother in disbelief.

"Come on," she said. "I'll start, you join in. . . . *I'm ti-i-i-i-red and I don't wanna go to the bloody school board meeting! It always lasts too long, and we never get anything accomplished. Ever! Do I haaaave to go? Do I?"*

She looked at me.

"Join me," she said. "It's quite cathartic, actually."

"*Do I haaaave to?*" we whined in unison.

"Ho ho ho?" asked my father.

I turned. He had rolled up right behind us without our even noticing.

"Private joke, ducks," said my mother.

She kissed the top of his head, then winked at me.

"There's hamburger meat in the fridge, along with salad fixings," she said, picking up her file folder and plucking the car keys from the hook on the wall. She made her way toward the mudroom and then the door. "Don't worry about the dishes," she called. "As for meds: I've written instructions and put them by his pills. And, in any event, he knows what he takes."

I followed her into the mudroom. My mother reached for the doorknob.

"Mom," I said. "Are you sure about this?"

"Angelina, dear," said my mother, pulling her hand from the doorknob and taking my chin between thumb and forefinger, "you have helped him pee. You are more than qualified for the position."

"But you've always been in the house when I've taken care of Dad," I said. "And I've never put him to bed before."

"You'll be fine, Angelina," she said. "Besides, there are no budget items on the agenda, so I may be back in less than three hours. Hold the thought."

She kissed me lightly on the forehead, then opened the door and went outside.

"You know," I called after her, "if we had cell phones, I could call you in case of a problem."

"That's certainly true, love," said my mother.

"So you'll get me one?" I yelled after her as she walked across the driveway.

"No," said my mother. "But the fact that I won't get you one does not affect the truth of your statement."

She blew me a kiss and got into her car. I stood in the doorway and watched her close the car door, start the car, switch on the headlights, throw the car into reverse, look out the back window, throw the car into park, get out of the car, pick up Mokey, hand him to me, get back into the car, throw the car into reverse, look out the back window, back up, turn around, and drive off.

Mokey squirmed in my arms. Taking a deep breath of the night air, I quit stalling and brought him inside.

"So," I said to my father when I got back to the kitchen, "should we make dinner?" My voice was so bogusly cheerful I sounded like my sister. Yipes.

I opened the fridge and pulled out the chopped meat and salad stuff.

"We need a little music," I said. I turned on the radio and tuned in to the oldies station. Mama Cass was belting out "Words of Love."

I poured him a glass of red wine, and we began making dinner.

I put the chopped meat in a bowl and contemplated the spice rack. I reached for the salt and black pepper. I was about to shake some salt into the bowl when I felt my father's hand on my arm. I looked at him. He pointed to the cayenne pepper and dried parsley on the rack. I took those down. He took the parsley and tapped my arm with it. I held my hand out, palm up, and my father shook some parsley into it. I put that in the bowl.

My father did the same thing with every seasoning we were using and made sure I washed my hands well with soap after adding the cayenne pepper.

After that he guided me through the salad process. He pointed to the garlic, held up one finger, and pointed to the wooden salad bowl. He pointed to the garlic again, held up two fingers, then made the universal sign for "a little" with his thumb and forefinger, then pointed to the cruet. One clove of garlic to be rubbed on the bowl. Two small cloves for the dressing.

We were communicating.

"Dad," I said, "would you teach me how to make your famous garlic potatoes?"

He nodded.

I opened the potato drawer and looked at my father.

He held up four fingers.

I took four potatoes from the bag, washed them, and peeled them.

My father held the knife and guided my hand as I cut the first potato into pieces of the perfect size and shape. I did the other three by myself.

He used the universal "stop" gesture to tell me when I'd poured enough oil into the skillet and when the flame under the burner had reached the perfect height.

He shook the seasonings into my palm, and I added them to the potatoes in the skillet.

He used the rhythmic pat-on-the-arm method to tell me when to flip them, and he nodded when they were done.

I served up dinner and carried the plates to the table, and we sat down to eat. When he speared a potato on his fork and raised it to his mouth, I pretended to bite my nails.

He chewed slowly, with his eyes closed.

I waited.

He opened his eyes, licked his lips, and smiled. He reached into the breakfront behind him and pulled out another wine glass. He poured a small amount of red wine into it and handed it me. We raised our glasses, and he said, "Ho *ho* ho ho ho ho *ho*!"

We clinked our glasses together.

"The chef accepts your compliments!" I said, and we sipped.

After dinner we watched TV in Dad's room. I gave him the remote and lay down on my stomach on his big bed. Mokey jumped up to lie beside me.

My father flipped through a bunch of stations. A *Buffy the Vampire Slayer* rerun showed up on one channel.

"Stop!" I said.

My father ignored me and kept on surfing.

"No," I said, reaching for the remote. "Let's watch *Buffy*."

My father held the remote out of my reach.

"Ho ho ho ho," he said.

"You won't like it?" I said. "Is that what you're saying?"

He nodded.

"How do you know if you don't try it?" I asked him. My father raised his eyebrows. "Ho ho ho," he said.

"You just know?" I said, raising my eyebrows back at him.

He nodded again.

And then it hit me.

"Hey, Dad!" I said, sitting up and totally upsetting Mokey. "I understood Andrea-speak!"

My father nodded, then shook my hand solemnly in congratulations. Mokey jumped into his lap and yapped. I smiled proudly.

It was a total Disney moment.

To celebrate, he allowed me to watch *Buffy*. And just for the record, he totally loved it.

After the show ended, my father took his meds and

brushed his teeth, and we were like a well-oiled machine when it came to peeing. But getting him into bed proved to be a problem.

My dad might have lost weight since the stroke, but he was still a grown man, and I was still a sixteen-year-old girl in so-so shape. We had to test out several approaches to his bed before we were successful.

First he leaned on me to raise himself from the wheel-chair, but we were too far from the bed. So he sat back down and I wheeled him closer, and his footrests and feet ended up under the bed, and his knees hit the box spring, and I couldn't get in to help him stand.

When we finally calculated and achieved the perfect distance from the bed, and I'd gotten him, once again, to his feet, his foot caught on one of the footrests and he pitched forward, taking me with him. We landed half on the bed, half off, and it was really hard to get him onto the bed. I was scared. I couldn't quite support him, and he couldn't quite do it on his own: not enough resistance from the mattress to let him push himself up.

"I'm sorry, Dad," I said.

He shook his head and indicated it wasn't my fault.

I pulled the wheelchair toward us with my foot, then

put on the brakes. I draped his bad arm over my shoulder, and he used the wheelchair's armrest to hoist himself to a standing position, and then, slowly, we turned so his back was to the bed, and he sat down.

We were sweating and sat together for a minute, collecting ourselves and just, you know, breathing.

He lay back. I lifted his legs to the bed, then realized I had not pulled down the covers.

I pulled the covers down on the opposite side, helped my father roll over to that side, then pulled the covers down on the side he had just left, then helped him roll back. I pulled the covers up over him and sat down beside him. We looked at each other. I noticed a little bit of drool at the corner of his mouth. I hesitated only a moment before I wiped it away with the hem of my shirt.

My father looked at me, smiled, closed his eyes, and turned away.

I lay down beside him and put my arm over his shoulders.

"*Ti amo, Dad,*" I whispered.

When my mother came home several hours later, she found us asleep just like that: my father on his side under the blanket, me on top of the blanket with my arm thrown over my father's back.

She later told me that she'd stood there for a long time watching us and crying quietly in the dark.

The Winter Concert

The *night of the winter* concert was cold and cloudy. We dressed my father in a new shirt and pants and his sad white running shoes. Together my mother and I maneuvered my father out of the house and into the car, folded his wheelchair, and stowed it in the trunk. When he was settled in the front seat, I climbed into the back, and we drove off.

By the time we got to the school, it was snowing. My mother pulled the car up to the front of the school, and we reversed the process: I took the wheelchair out of the trunk, unfolded it, helped my mother unfold my father and maneuver him back into the wheelchair, then pushed him up the path to the front door while my mother went to park the car.

Into the entrance hall. A small table had been set up

outside the office, and it was stacked with programs. Mrs. Principal stood beside it, handing them out.

"Andrea!" said Mrs. Principal, hugging the programs under her arm and clasping the left hand he extended to her in both her hands. "So glad you could make it."

She sounded and looked genuinely happy.

My father smiled.

Mrs. Principal handed him a program and said, "We made a spot just for you. First row center aisle. You'll see it."

We wheeled into the cafeteria, which had been set up for the concert with a small sectional stage erected in the corner and folding chairs arranged in rows.

Two seats had been removed in the first row center, just as Mrs. P. had said, and Billy T. was standing in the space. He was wearing his school custodian duds: a white T-shirt, jeans, and work boots. His pager and cell hung from his belt in their leather holsters.

"I wasn't sure," he said as we pulled up, "if you'd need a two- or two-and-a-half chair space."

We backed my dad in, and I set the brake. We draped his jacket over the seat next to him to save it for my mother.

"I see two just about does it," said Billy T. "I'll make a note for future productions."

His pager beeped, and he checked the number.

"Gotta take this one," he said.

"EMT?" I asked.

"No," he replied. "Dorcas." He turned to my father. "Great to have you here, Andrea," he said. He gripped my father's shoulder, then pulled out his cell and punched in a speed dial and walked away.

Jax's mom came running up and planted a kiss on each of his cheeks.

"*Bon soir!*" she said. "*Bienvenu!*" Tears were coursing down her cheeks. Her husband shook my father's hand gruffly and cleared his throat.

Granny Nancy grasped both my father's hands. She was dressed like she'd just stepped out of Woodstock, with a long batik skirt and a fringed shawl hanging over her shoulders. Her faded red hair hung straight. Her earrings were dream catchers with real feathers, a rose tattoo climbed out of the sleeve of her peasant shirt, and she wore a big turquoise ring on the thumb of her left hand. She was plump and pretty and smelled of patchouli.

"*Quel* bummer," she said to my father. "I send you positive vibes, man."

My father gave her the peace sign.

Word of my father's appearance had spread, and soon he was surrounded by a small crowd. Everyone was glad to see him. He smiled and shook hands with them all.

Mrs. Percy broke through the crowd and stood beside the wheelchair. She was dressed in her bathrobe and had her hair up in curlers. Her bare feet were stuffed into her hiking boots.

"I'm going straight to bed after this," she said by way of explanation. She gave my father a voucher for a free coffee and doughnut. "There are few things in this world that a visit to a diner can't make a little better."

"Ho, ho!" said my father, bobbing his head in a little courtesy gesture.

"Gotta go, Daddy," I said, kissing him on the cheek. "Will you be okay?"

He nodded.

"'Ee'll be okay," said Mrs. T. "I will stay wit 'im until your mozer arrives."

I noticed Celeste standing in the doorway, staring at my father. She distracted me, and because I wasn't paying attention, I took a step and bumped into my father's chair. His carryall pouch came loose from its Velcro moorings and landed on the floor, where one of his just-in-case

Depends fell out and lay there for all the world to see.

I saw Celeste stare at it.

I waited for her to laugh or smirk.

Instead she studied me, then pulled her head out of the doorway and disappeared from sight. I just stood there, paralyzed.

Mrs. T. picked up the diaper and stuffed it back into the sack, which she re-Velcroed to the chair. She patted me on the shoulder and gave me a little shove.

"Jacques is waiting for you," she said.

I walked off slowly. When I got to the doorway, I looked back at my father. He still had a large crowd around him, and here came my mother, accompanied by Liz, smiling, greeting, but inexorably making her way to my father's side like an icebreaker plowing the frozen Arctic seas.

I headed toward the music room. Most of the rest of the chorus was already there. Jax sat on a desk with his feet on a chair and motioned me over.

I held up one finger in the universal sign for "just a sec" and looked around for Celeste. She was lounging against the far wall in black trousers, a button-down white shirt, and black clogs. Her hair was loose and fell softly around her face. It struck me that she looked more like a Celeste than I'd ever seen her look before. She looked almost pretty.

But I still didn't want to be her girlfriend.

I walked boldly up to her.

"I'm sorry about what I said at the diner," I said. "It was stupid. I was nervous."

Celeste nodded.

"And you know what you said about could we?" I continued. "Well, I think we could. Be friends, I mean."

She looked at me then to be sure I wasn't baiting her. Then she offered me a small smile. I smiled back.

"What was that about?" asked Jax when I sat down beside him.

"Oh, just a little preconcert bonding," I said.

Mr. C. came into the room. He was wearing a neat black suit, very Armani, and no tie.

"Where's your tie, Mr. C.?" asked Jax, who looked smart in tan chinos, a blue oxford shirt, and a tweedy vest.

"Collarless shirt, Mr. Tatro," said Mr. C. "Height of fashion. But I'm not entirely pop-culture-free."

He opened his jacket to reveal Jayhawk suspenders. "Rock chalk Jayhawk, go KU," he said.

A small, creamy envelope fell to the floor. He picked it up and put it in his inside breast pocket.

"Whoa!" said Jason. "What's that? A top secret document?"

"Totally classified information, Mr. Andrews," said Mr. C. "You'd have to achieve a much higher level of security clearance before I could reveal the contents to you."

Mr. C. rapped the desk with his little baton.

"Okay, ladies and gentlemen," he said. "It's showtime!"

We lined up and walked toward the cafeteria. In the hall Mr. C. fell into step beside me.

"Glad your dad could make it," he said to me.

I nodded.

We entered the cafeteria and climbed up onto the stage. When we had taken our places, Mr. C. made his way to the mike.

"Friends, family, community members with nothing else to do tonight," he said, "thank you for coming to the Blodgett High School winter concert. As you all know by now, we are presenting an all–Andrew Lloyd Webber program, including selections from *Jesus Christ Superstar*, *Phantom of the Opera*, and *Evita*. The singers worked hard to put this recital together, and I'm proud of them. I think you will be too. But before we begin, I'd like to welcome a valued community member and fellow ardent A.L.W. fan back home, and dedicate this concert to him: Mr. Andrea Rossini."

Everyone clapped. Then someone stood, and soon everyone was standing. My father looked around, blinked his eyes, then smiled and lifted his left hand in a salute of acknowledgment.

When the ovation ended, Mr. C. said, "Now, sit back, relax, and enjoy the show." The overhead lights were dimmed and the stage lights lit. Mr. C. sat down at his piano and struck the first few chords of the introduction. My heart sped up like it does before every concert, and then we began to sing.

There was nothing to worry about. We were totally fabulous. We moved magically through the medley, right through to the grand finale. When Celeste stepped forward and took the mike, a hush filled the room. Mr. C. played the introduction, and she began to sing. Her angelic voice filled the air, and we were all transfixed by the beauty of it. She lifted us out of the ranks of rural high school recital and into a whole other sphere entirely.

And then something happened that will live on in the history of our school—and Blodgett—possibly forever.

As Celeste moved into the final chorus, her voice was joined by a familiar tenor voice.

It was my father.

"Don't cry for me, Angelina!
The truth is I shall not leave you.
All through my wild days,
My mad existence,
I kept my promise,
Don't keep your distance."

Yes, he said "Angelina," but it didn't matter. Not really. He sang the other words flawlessly, and his rich, resonant voice and her clear, high voice came together to form a harmonic blend that was truly ethereal.

When they finished, the room was silent. No rustle of paper. No hiss of someone sliding into a jacket. Not even a cough. It was so quiet you could almost hear the snow fall.

Mr. C. was the first to break the trance. He stood up from his bench and began to applaud. Soon we all joined in. My father looked around and smiled. My mother looked at her lap and cried. Celeste bowed her head. And I stepped off the risers and went to stand with my parents.

Killer finale, huh?

When we left the school that night, the snow had stopped, but there was a slippery layer on the school's steep driveway. My mother went to get the car, and we pushed my father sloppily through the slush and stowed him in the front seat. We crept slowly down the steep incline, sliding and skidding in a frightening way. In front of us Mrs. Percy's Saturn skidded sideways and hit the Andrewses' car, which was parked at the side of the road. No one was hurt, but they had to wait for Frank, our town mechanic and historical-society president, to take his family home from the concert, change, and drive back with the tow truck.

Even so, Mrs. Percy gave my dad a thumbs-up as we slipped past her, to the bottom of the drive.

As we drove along the main road, I leaned over the back of the front seat to speak to my father.

"Daddy," I said. "You sang all the words. Can you say something else?"

My mother and I waited expectantly.

"Ho ho," he said.

And you know, he never actually spoke another word again.

Last Day on Earth

❧❧❧

My *father's last day on Earth* started out in the usual way—and it's amazing to me that I can even use the word "usual" in connection with the life we had with my father after his stroke. But, in fact, things did become usual in their own unusual way.

You can get used to anything, I guess.

My father woke early. My mother had spent the night in his room—something she had been doing more frequently. I wonder now, in looking back, if she had a feeling or something. You know, about how time was short. I tried to keep myself from thinking about my father's future at all, which, when I did think about it, appeared to have only two possible scenarios:

1. *He would remain largely just as he was for years and*
years, and we would just have to keep on coping and secretly
hoping for a miracle we'd long since begun to doubt, or
2. *He would die.*

You see why I would do my best to avoid looking ahead.

Anyway.

On that particular morning I came downstairs to find my father seated in the dining room. The scene looked familiar, but I couldn't help thinking, *What's wrong with this picture?* and then it hit me: He was dressed in the same nightshirt and sitting in the exact same spot he'd been standing in on the day he'd had his stroke. The spot where Mokey had peed on him from above. I had a time-warp moment and actually saw him there laughing, with the pee dripping down his face and into the hairy channels of his beard.

I closed my eyes and realigned my time zones in the dark, then opened them and walked over and planted a kiss on his cheek. I remember the sensation of his skin on my lips—dry and brittle, but soft, too. It was a different kind of softness than a baby's cheek: looser, kind of like tissue paper.

I loved him a lot at that moment.

We all had breakfast together, and my mom was in a great mood.

"So, Andrea," she said, "what shall we do today, eh? Icicle removal? Some snow sculptures? A bit of forestry with the chainsaw, perhaps?"

I almost choked. "What?" I said.

"Oh, I won't do the actual chainsaw work," said my mother. "I'll support your father from behind, and he'll use his good hand to take down some of the low branches on the footpath."

My father made a muscle with his good arm and cocked his head confidently.

"Mom! Are you serious? That is just so dangerous. . . ."

And they both burst out laughing.

I looked from one to the other, and they seemed so pleased with themselves, with their joke, that I couldn't help but laugh too.

"For grown-ups," I said, "you guys are total juveniles. What, are you channeling your inner second-grade boys?"

The bus horn honked. I jumped up, grabbed my book bag, and ran out, shouting, "Later!" over my shoulder.

Wish I'd turned around to have another look.

*   *   *

When we pulled into the school driveway, Mrs. Principal was waiting at the entrance, and I just knew: I knew that sometime between the time I'd left my house and the time I'd arrived at school my father had died. I didn't find out until later that he'd had a massive heart attack and died almost instantly on the bedroom floor.

While I sat in Mrs. P.'s office, I tried to figure out exactly what I had been doing the very minute that my father had died. I must not be psychic, because I had no clue. I had not felt a flash of pain or disorientation during my conversation with Ben, a first grader on the route. When we passed Jax's house and I saw him in his truck, I was not visited by a ghostly premonition. When the bus turned into the driveway of the school, I did not feel icy fingers closing around my heart.

So when was it?

I don't know.

I'll never know.

I hate that.

Anyway.

Mrs. Principal herself drove me back home. It was a quiet ride.

I went in and found my mother and Liz in their assigned seats. No coffee. Not that kind of morning. Tea, though, and it smelled like comfort. My mother rested her forehead on her hand, and her elbow on the table. She was crying. I actually saw a tear slide down her nose, dangle on the tip for a moment as if in indecision, then drop into her teacup, dead center.

Liz sat quietly, watching her and holding her free hand. She looked up when I appeared, and smiled but said nothing. She reached out and took one of my hands. I sat down across from my mother and reached out with my other hand to touch her hand. She took that hand away from her face and looked at me with such deep sorrow that I began to cry too. She took my hand and held it, and all three of us held hands and cried together.

And even after our tears had stopped, we stayed there at the table holding hands for a long, long time.

Not a Church

❧✿❧

In our small town is a well-known place called Goodchild Hall. It was once a church, but it's not a church anymore. It was bought up by the Blodgett Historical Society and lovingly restored, and now it houses the Blodgett Museum of History (two glass cases with mostly old photos of town figures outfitted for various wars, and the Purple Heart won by Gordon Jewett in World War II). The historical society makes the hall available for weddings and concerts, Town Market Day, and the occasional memorial service.

The first memorial service I can remember being at was for Jax's great-grandfather, who died in his sleep one night. Since then I've been at Denise Tetreault's, who died of brain cancer; Private First Class Scotty Lumbra's, who died in Iraq; and Buddy Pittman's, aka Dr. Drain, a master plumber, who died while riding his bike one brilliant summer morning between East Blodgett and Blodgett Center. The number of people at his service set new town records, as yet unbroken.

The day of my father's memorial service was brilliant, too: one of those New England late-autumn days that give the season its well-deserved rep. The sky was a blue so sharp you could cut your eye on it. The leaves were so splendid that a colossal number of flatlander leaf peepers passed through town as we filed into and later out of the little clapboard ex-church, giving them a look at authentic northern-Vermont life in addition to foliage. At no extra charge.

I set up a bulletin board on an easel just inside the door. Along the top I wrote:

Andrea Rossini
1934 – 2003

And I stuck up my favorite photos that included my father. There was the one I had taken of my mother and him walking down the road holding hands on a winter day. There was the one of him and me at the café in Italy.

There was the one of him and Francesca, and the one of me and him that had been on his dresser. There was the one of him skiing and another of him holding his grandson when he was an infant while the proud mother, Francesca, looked on. There was the one of him in a long white dress in his mother's arms. There was the one of him standing with me and Sugar that day we won the Catch Sugar contest, and there was, of course, the one of him brandishing the pizza slicer.

Oh. And there was the one I took of him and Mom on the day we shoveled the porch. My sister took issue with this one.

"Why do you want to put that one up?" she hissed. "Who wants to remember him that way?"

"I do," I said.

Anthony looked at the picture.

"Why don't you like it, Mom?" he asked.

"He's in a wheelchair," she said. "He looks old."

"He looks happy," said Anthony.

Francesca looked at her son, then studied the picture.

"You're right, Anthony," she said, putting an arm around him. "He does look happy."

"He was a great grandpa," said Anthony.

"He was a great father, too," I said, feeling the tears pricking the insides of my eyelids.

Anthony kissed me on the cheek, then went to sit beside his father, who was fiddling with his Palm Pilot.

My sister put her arm around my shoulders.

"It's harder for you than for him," she said. "Losing a grandfather first is at least the right sequence. Losing a father at your age throws things out of alignment."

"What about losing a father at your age?" I asked.

"Not so unexpected," she said, and I saw the tears glistening in her eyes. "Still hard, though."

We hugged each other, then my sister went to sit with her family.

I volunteered to speak first, so as everyone settled into seats, I climbed the two steps to the stage and stood behind the podium. The room was packed; there was hardly standing room. People stood in the aisles and leaned back against the walls. The doors were jammed with people. I saw Mrs. Percy, dressed in a respectful pale yellow Jackie O. suit, white gloves with buttons at the wrists, a small yellow Jackie O. hat with a net veil that fell over her face to just below her nose, and on her feet her trademark hiking boots.

My mother sat up front next to Liz, nodding and thanking people who came to speak to her: Billy T. and Dorcas; Mrs. Principal, Mr. C., and most of the other teachers from school; Jason, Celeste, and Walker; James and Annika. They all filed solemnly into seats, filling them from the front to the back.

Jax and his family sat in the last row. Granny Nancy was beautiful in a loose-fitting white linen dress. She sat next to the members of the school board, who were sandwiched by the two warring postmistresses. Not even the death of Andrea Rossini could stay these two from their appointed hostilities.

This thought made me smile—and I realized that it was a perfect time to get things started.

"Hi," I said, and then waited for quiet. "Thank you all for coming today to celebrate and commemorate the life of my father, Andrea Rossini. My father was a man who loved life. He loved it and, more important, he wasn't afraid of it. I think that's what I admired most about him. I will miss his laugh. I will miss his voice. I will even miss him yelling at me when at least *I* thought I did not deserve it. But what I will miss most is the way he anchored our family. After he had the stroke, I was afraid that our family would fall apart. But even without words my father held our family together, and the three of us learned a new way to be together. I think we are stronger for it."

And here I began to cry. I looked at my mother. Tears were coursing down her cheeks, but she was smiling at me at the same time.

I took a minute or two to sturdy myself, then continued. "Laila once told me that fall is a Vermont bus driver's heaven: no mud, no ice, just dry roads in need of a little grading. I have found myself thinking about what heaven might be for my father. I think his heaven is a place where there are dirt roads and skiing, and Dante on the nightstand. It's a place where he can look at the stars, drink good wine, and have an appreciative audience for his every opinion." A wave of laughter rippled through the crowd.

I paused for a moment, putting off saying the words I'd tried hard not to say until now. But it was time. "Goodbye, Dad," I said. "*Ti voglio bene.*"

I took a deep breath, wiped my cheeks, then walked down the stairs. Liz stood and started for the stage, meeting me at the bottom of the steps. She nodded at me once, then she climbed the stairs, and I took a seat beside my mother, who put her arm around me. I saw the tears dripping slowly down her cheeks. She did not look at me or make a sound.

Liz stood behind the podium. She looked strong and dignified, her black-and-white hair in a loose braid that hung over her left shoulder, her strong and small body in loose-fitting, well-tailored black trousers, a white silk shirt tucked into the waistband, a red leather belt around her waist. Her shoes were red too, and she had on a bit of red lipstick.

"Andrea Rossini," she began. "Some people loved him. Some people didn't like him. But nobody didn't know who he was."

We laughed in agreement. Liz raised her eyebrows at us all and smiled.

"Andrea was my friend," she said. "He was generous, irascible, hospitable, and opinionated." She paused. "He was impatient but, more important, he was not intolerant."

She took us all in with a sweep of her head, then shifted her gaze to the view that could be seen through a clear pane in the stained-glass window just between Jesus and Mary Magdalene. We all looked too, though most of us knew what she was looking at: the barn wall across the road that sported a large sign that said TAKE BACK VERMONT.

She turned back to us.

"This is a great legacy for a father to leave his child," she said, looking at me. "And one we can all benefit from. I will miss you, Andrea."

She stepped down, took a seat beside me, and reached for my hand.

After that Mrs. Percy recalled how my father had always brought everyone in to play Catch Sugar and what a big tipper he'd been—and she had to reach up under her veil to dab at her eyes with a small, white, lace-edged handkerchief. Mrs. Principal spoke of his work on the school board, and Jax's father told the story of the time my father drove our tractor into the woods in the spring and sank the frickin' thing into the mud halfway up the big back wheels because the ground was still too frickin' soft to drive such a heavy piece of equipment on, and how he'd had to come up with a come-along and some big logs to get him out.

"Andrea was a little guy, but he jumped right into the frickin' mud and shoved a log right under the wheel, and darn if that tractor didn't rise up out of that mud with a huge suckin' noise." Jax's father shook his head in sheer appreciation. So did Sean and Lucien. Jax hid his face in his hand, and his mother just smiled with her lips closed.

Lastly, Mr. C. took the podium. He was wearing a Godzilla tie and looked solemn, but there was the ghost of a smile playing around his lips. What was he up to?

"We all know what a rabid Andrew Lloyd Webber fan Andrea was," he said. "Well, after he had his stroke, I wrote a letter to the big guy himself inviting him to attend our concert. It was Andrea's suggestion."

"I got a response. I had planned to read it after the concert, but, well, you all know what happened, and so it turned out to be bad timing, and if there's one thing seventeen years in showbiz has taught me, it's that timing is everything."

We laughed.

"Anyway, I'd like to read it now," he said. He pulled an envelope from his inside jacket pocket, slipped the card out of it, put on his reading glasses, and read:

*"Dear Mr. Crispi and the Students of Blodgett
High School,*

*Thank you for your kind invitation to hear the
Blodgett High School chorus sing a medley of my work.
I am unable to attend, but I wanted to tell the students
there that it is concerts like theirs that are the true
measure of the success of my work. And to Andrea
Rossini, who you suggest just might be my biggest fan
north of the forty-fifth parallel—a dubious distinction
at best—I want to say good luck.*

*Best regards,
Andrew Lloyd Webber."*

Mr. C. looked up from the card.

"Good luck from me, too, Andrea," he said. "We're not crying for you. The truth is, you'll never leave us."

After the service we all went back to our house to eat. The back doors were open, so Jax and I took our plates out to the patio and sat on the step.

"Great service," he said.

"Think there were as many people as there were for Dr. Drain?" I asked him.

"Definitely," he said.

"Me too," I said.

We chewed in silence for a while.

"I need a drink," I said, standing. "You?"

"Coke," he said.

I put my plate on the step and went into the house. As I crossed the room to the counter where the drinks were, I noticed my mother standing by the window in the living room, looking lost. Deflated. I took a step toward her, then saw Liz approach her from the other side of the room. I stepped back into the hall where I couldn't be seen but could still hear what they were saying. Yet another rule of thumb when eavesdropping: Stay out of sight.

Liz touched my mother's shoulder.

"Nicola?" she said. "You okay?"

My mother turned to face Liz. She looked distraught.

"I was short with him," she said. "Sometimes I lost my patience. Sometimes I wished he would die. And now . . . now I feel some relief."

She sobbed, then put her head on Liz's shoulder and just wept. Liz held her and rubbed her back for a long time in silence. When my mother had regained her composure, Liz lifted my mother's face, took a clean white handkerchief out of her pocket, and gently dabbed the tears off her cheeks. Then she placed a hand on each of my mother's shoulders, looked her straight in the eyes, and said, "You took care of him responsibly and well. You never shirked your duty. You have nothing to feel guilty about."

My mother looked at Liz through the tears that still clung to her eyelashes. And then I saw her shoulders relax as she accepted the truth of what Liz had said. Then my mother leaned forward and kissed Liz on the lips.

After that my mother straightened up, squared her shoulders, walked to the bar, and poured herself a drink.

Meanwhile, I stood in that dark hallway and let the tears fall.

Life After Death

In *post-Andrea world* *my* mother and I have not yet
worked out how to navigate the space where my
father isn't.

It's another paradox: absence and presence.

My father's absence is a huge presence in our lives.

And its effect on my mother and me is unpredictable.
Sometimes we are reminded of him and it draws us
together. Other times we go for each other's throats.

This morning, for example.

I met my mother, as usual, in the kitchen. She was not
sitting at the table. Instead she was wedged into the corner where one counter meets another, leaning on an
elbow and holding a mug of coffee in her hands. Since
my father's death there have been times when she seems
really distant; this was one of those times.

"Good morning, Mom," I said.

She nodded at me but didn't say anything.

She watched me put my bag down and make myself some oatmeal. When I was little, my father always made it for me and I always helped him. I used to kneel on a chair at his side at the counter, and we would prepare cereal, him in his flannel nightshirt, barefoot, me in my Princess Jasmine pajamas, ballet shoes, and occasionally a pair of swim goggles.

Hey, what can I say? I've always had style.

"Order, temperature, moderation. These are the three things that separate a good oatmeal from a truly great oatmeal, *cara mia*," my father said one time, assembling the ingredients and tools and putting them on the counter. I measured one cup of rolled oats while my father got the two cups of water and poured them into the pot. He covered the pot, turned the burner on, and leaned his head down to adjust the flame to the perfect height.

Because a watched pot never boils, we did not watch.

Instead we put out our place mats, poured ourselves our drinks, laid out spoons, and put the maple syrup between us. Billy T.'s syrup, I might add. Family-run sugarhouse, third generation. I went to his sugarhouse during boiling season once. I remember it was steamy and sweet-smelling and cozy, and that the hot dogs they cooked in the boiling sap tasted like candy.

Anyway.

Back to the oatmeal.

By that time the water was boiling. My father let me pour in the oats while he stirred. Then he added a pinch of salt from the saltcellar, scooped a bit of butter from its dish, and stuck it in the cereal, swirling lightly until the butter melted. Then he handed the wooden spoon to me.

"Now we watch, *cara mia*, until the oats, water, butter, and salt become oatmeal," he said.

I stirred solemnly until the cereal reached the consistency we liked—somewhere between done and not quite done; chewy but not hard, smooth but not slimy.

"What do you think?" my father asked me. "Is it done?"

I regarded the cereal.

"One more minute," I decided.

Now, at that age I was not known for my keen sense of time. When I was about three my father told me it was my bedtime in ten minutes, and I said, "No! Nine!"

"You drive a hard bargain," my father replied, "but nine it is."

It's a true story.

"Let's see if you're right," said my father, setting the kitchen timer for one minute. I kept stirring. When the buzzer buzzed, my father flipped the burner off, then lifted the pot and divided the cereal between the two bowls. We carried our bowls to the table, added a little maple syrup, and took our first bite. My father rolled the oatmeal on his tongue, chewed it slowly, and swallowed.

"I believe, *cara mia*," said my father, "that one minute was exactly right. What do you think?"

"Perfect," I said.

At this point you're probably wondering where my mother was. Sleeping. Saturday mornings my father and I had a breakfast date. Just the two of us.

But I digress. Now back to the original story.

My mother sipped her coffee and watched me measure the oats; measure and pour the water into the pot; adjust the flame; put my place mat, the syrup, and a spoon on the table; pour myself a drink; add the oats to the boiling water while I stirred; add a pat of butter and a pinch of salt; stir and stir; then flip the flame off and serve myself a bowl of oatmeal.

I sat down at the table.

"Your father taught you well," my mother observed.

I looked at her. The words were complimentary, but the tone was not.

"Too bad he didn't also teach you to offer to make enough for other people too," she said.

"What? Excuse me, but I thought I was helping by taking care of myself!" I snapped. "I thought you'd be glad I could do it myself so you wouldn't have to be bothered. But instead you criticize me?"

A moment passed.

"I *expect* you to take care of yourself, Angelina," she said quietly, "you're sixteen."

I stood up, oatmeal forgotten, grabbed my backpack, and banged out of the house.

"I don't want to go home," I told Jax after school that afternoon. "My mother and I had a huge fight, and I just don't feel like seeing her right now."

Jax stopped the truck. "Where do you want to go?" he asked.

"I want to go to Laura's barn," I said.

"It'll be muddy," he said.

"Bring on the mud," I said, holding up a hiking-booted foot. "My Manolo Blahnik trail shoes are made for mud."

He pulled over and parked. We got out of the truck, and I followed him into the woods just below my house.

Laura's barn isn't really Laura's barn. It isn't really even a barn. Not anymore. It's the stone foundation of a barn. Jax and I used to play there as kids.

We slogged through the mud on the overgrown carriage road that led to the barn's entrance. Fiddleheads and skunk cabbage tips were breaking through the earth in bursts of green.

I stepped through the space between the stones where the door once was. A copse of young popple trees grew in the center. Last year's leaves—deep, slick, and wet—carpeted the floor. There was a bit of snow in the north corner. A shaft of sunlight came through the bare branches and shone on a wooden plank that Jax and I had put across two stones to make a bench.

I sat down on it and leaned back against the stone foundation, which was still a bit warm from the afternoon sunshine. I closed my eyes and let the sun make color bursts on the inside of my eyelids.

Suddenly a shadow came between me and the sun. I

opened my eyes to see if it was a cloud. It wasn't.

It was Jax. In a bonnet.

"Manly!" I said in my best Laura voice. "Why ever are you wearin' my bonnet?"

"Because, my dear Laura, I want to *be* you, and I could not fit into your frock!"

We laughed. He sat down beside me.

"Where'd you find this?" I said, pulling the bonnet off his head. It was old and dirty and familiar; I tried it on.

"It was between the two loose rocks in the foundation, just where we left it," said Jax, sitting down beside me.

"Did you really want to be Laura all those times we played *The First Four Years*?" I asked.

"I don't know," he said, taking the bonnet and putting it back on his head. He tied a lovely bow just under his right ear. "I can't really remember." He shrugged. "Probably." He took a breath. "So, what happened between your mom and you this morning?"

I told him about the oatmeal incident.

"She's stressed out," he said.

"She's not the only one," I said. "Now that my father's gone, I feel like I don't have anyone who really understands me anymore." I felt the tears start to well up. Again.

"You have me," he said. "I'm here for you, Ange."

"Thanks, Jax," I said. And I leaned over to kiss him on the cheek.

Only he turned his head, so I ended up kissing him on the lips.

And he slipped me some tongue.

I pulled back and looked at him.

"Hey!" I said. "What's going on here?"

"I thought you would like it," he said.

"What about what *you* like?" I asked.

He folded his hands in his lap and studied them. "You looked so sad—and I thought that what you liked could be more important than what *I* liked right now," he said.

I took one of his hands in mine.

"Jax Tatro," I said, "that's the nicest thing any boy has ever said to me."

And then I told him about my talk with Celeste and how I understood our situation, his and mine, so much better now.

"We'll just have to wait for our own Mr. Rights," I said to him. "Together."

Jax smiled and fiddled with the ribbon on the bonnet.

"I just hope," I added, "that when I find mine, he'll look half as good in a bonnet as you do."

Later on Jax dropped me off at home. I hopped out of the truck and walked over to the driver's-side window.

"Are we okay?" I asked him.

He looked at me.

"We're always okay," he said.

He backed out of the driveway, and when he got to the end, he turned and waved. I waved back, he drove away, and I went into the house.

I found my mother in the kitchen, listening to Mozart, sitting in dim light.

I put down my book bag.

"Mom," I said. "I'm sorry about this morning."

She turned to look at me, wiping her hands on her apron.

"Sit down, Angelina," she said.

I sat.

"I have been thinking about our row all day," she said.

She sat down across the table from me and took my hand in both of hers.

"Angelina," she said, "my darling Angelina." And she

sighed. "I don't think you know how dear you are to me, and this is because I don't think I show you in ways that you can understand. I am harsh because I expect a lot of you, and I don't think that's bad, but it must be balanced out with something else, and that's what I've neglected. My reasons are manifold and not relevant to this discussion, but, my love, my pet, I will try, as your father counseled, to look at who you are instead of who you aren't."

"When did Daddy tell you that?" I asked.

"A few weeks before he died," she said, and smiled at me. "You'd be surprised how much that man could express with his one-word lexicon.

"Actually," she added, "he showed me. He gave me this." She reached into her apron pocket and pulled out a small Carmex jar.

"Lip balm reminded you of how dear I am to you?" I asked. "I don't get it."

"Never judge a jar by its cover, love," said my mother. She unscrewed the lid and turned the jar so the contents—what appeared to be a dozen or more freshwater pearls—spilled out onto her place mat. "These are your baby teeth," said my mother. "I wrestled the tooth fairy to the ground to retain ownership of each one."

I picked up one of the small, white teeth and held it in the palm of my hand.

"A few of them split in half," she said, "but I Krazy-Glued them back together."

I closed my fingers around the small tooth and held it tight, then stood up and walked around the table and sat in my mother's lap. She held me and rocked me.

Now it's dark and late, and I am lying out here on Midnight Rock thinking about the day's events.

Tonight is the first night, in fact, that I have been back to Midnight Rock since my father died. Tonight, when I let Mokey out, I saw it, shining silvery in the moonlight, like a hole in the world, and I found myself heading across the driveway almost as if I were possessed. Up until now I hadn't been able to get near it; I just had to see it to start crying.

Anyway.

The rock is still warm from today's sun. I'm sitting here now, testing myself to see if I feel like crying.

I don't. So I take it up a notch: I lie down on Midnight Rock and look at the stars.

Still no tears.

Mokey comes and lays his head on my chest.

I still don't feel like crying, and I'm wondering about this when I hear the door open, and I sense my mother's silhouette in the doorframe. Mokey lifts his head to look but makes no move to leave me. I hear the crunching of the pea stone under her feet as she crosses the driveway, and the *susurrus* of her moving through the grass. I feel her standing over me, looking down, like she's deciding whether or not to join me.

Do I even want her to join me? This is our rock, after all, my father's and mine. Do I want to share?

It's not our sky, Angelina, I hear my father say.

I open my eyes.

"Would you like to join me?" I ask, looking up at my mother.

She presses her lips together and looks at me for a long time, then she says, "No, but thank you. Thank you for asking." Instead she offers me her hand. "Dance with me, Angelina."

Slowly I put my hand in hers, and she helps me up.

Then we dance.

As my mother hums "Waltz of the Flowers," we glide

around Midnight Rock while Mokey watches. The stars are pinpoints of ancient light, and the Milky Way spills, luminous, across the sky. The air smells green and rich and feels soft and cool, and I breathe it in, thinking this is what heaven must feel like.

Acknowledgments

The author would like to thank her daughter for sleeping late on Sunday mornings and being able to play by herself so well; Dan Gutman, twentieth-century coworker, for sharing with others; Sheree, Emma, and Claire Willis and Flora Jiang, whose comments helped shape the manuscript; Ruilong Hu, for a boy's perspective; Captain R. O. Heimbecker, for technical support in the North Country; The Jennifers (Jennifer Weiss, Jennifer Klonsky, and Jennifer Pricola) for asking the right questions, taking the helm in mid-ocean, and proofreading excellence, respectively; and, of course, the residents of Blodgett, Vermont. (You know who you are.)

Special recognition must go to Daniel, Marijke, and Suzanne, without whose humanity, courage, and devotion to each other this story could not have been.